Newspaper Murders

A Chicago Police Mystery

Joe Gash

G.K.HALL &CO.
Boston, Massachusetts
1987

1-0925

Published in Large Print by arrangement with
Holt, Rinehart and Winston.

G.K. Hall Large Print Book Series.

Set in 16 pt Plantin.

Library of Congress Cataloging in Publication Data

Gash, Joe.
  Newspaper murders.

  (G.K. Hall large print book series)
  1. Large type books. I. Title.
[PS3557.A8446N4 1987]   813'.54   86-19408
ISBN 0-8161-4219-X (lg. print)

For Jack Lane and Rat

The newspaper has no friends. Nor does it want any.

—*Remark attributed to J. Loy Maloney, newspaper editor in Chicago about 1950, when asked a favor by a "friendly" politician*

Author's Note

This is a story set in a real place, in a real
time. But it is fiction. Despite this, the
names of real streets, public buildings, taverns, restaurants, parks, and neighborhoods
are used.

From time to time in Chicago, there are
special squads or special teams set up between the state's attorney's office and the
Chicago police department, usually in re-
sponse to public pressure stage-managed by
the local news media.

At the time this novel is set, there were
four newspapers in Chicago.

The story of Jake Lingle, the disgraced
reporter with the *Chicago Tribune* who was
gunned to death in the Randolph Street station tunnel of the Illinois Central, is true as

told in these pages.

An attempt has been made to create, in a simple way, some sense of the pressures of life inside a newspaper office and the types of people who work for newspapers. But this is fiction again, and no attempt has been made to depict real people, living or dead.

It should also be pointed out that a number of black groups in the city have, from time to time, achieved notoriety and public notice for their activities. Some have been legitimate organizations, some have not.

Some of the dialogue is rough, some is racist. It is an attempt to mirror reality, not to judge it or alter it to suit particular times or individual mores. Some will be offended by this book because it is explicit in language and action. This notice is fair warning.

Media pressures have generated political hysteria from time to time. This phenomenon is not unique to Chicago. Nor is Chicago immune to it.

Newspaper
Murders

1

Leave Your Message

Six weeks before the murder, the telephone began to ring in the office of the managing editor. He was not in. It was two minutes past two in the morning and beyond the glass wall of the office, a copyboy was dozing at the city desk in the immense, low-ceilinged newsroom that stretched the length of the building.

Across the newsroom, near the wall where the chattering wire-service machines spewed their overnight reports, the overnight reporter—the unlucky one kept on duty "just in case"—stood chatting with the drama critic who had just finished her deadline review of a new play. The play had opened

1

that night at the Shubert Theater in the Loop and it would close within a week, devastated by bad reviews and bad box office. The play was a comedy.

The telephone rang twice in the office of the managing editor and then was answered by a tape-recording machine.

"Mr. Queeney is not in at the moment," said the taped voice of Miss Thompson, the woman who sat in the outer office during regular working hours. "Leave your message and your call will be acknowledged."

The wording of the recorded message came from Michael Queeney himself. Like Queeney, who was the managing editor, it was vague and vaguely pompous. Did the message imply that the call would be returned or did it imply that the message would even be listened to? Miss Thompson had pointed this out to Queeney but the managing editor had merely shrugged. The ambiguity pleased the editor in Queeney as well as the corporate career climber. He was not a man to make too many commitments unless he was sure of his overwhelming advantage. His caution had enabled him to survive when others had not.

He was the only holdover editor under

2

the new ownership. The new ownership had brought in brash, hard-hitting people from New York and elsewhere to reshape the "image" of the paper. The old, liberal ownership of the newspaper had tsked-tsked publicly and privately about the "new" people and their bloodthirsty style of journalism and then had quietly gone away several million dollars richer from the sale.

The old editor had resigned as well as the old publisher and the old city editor. Queeney had been expected to join them in upholding the sanctity of his journalism ethics. After all, Queeney had once won a Sigma Delta Chi award for his devotion to journalistic ideals.

Queeney did not feel there were many jobs left in journalism that were open to him, certainly not positions as powerful as being the managing editor of a top-tier newspaper in the second-largest American city. Not for men who were fifty-two years old. Even if they had a closet full of awards.

Queeney had swallowed his pride along with several fifths of Johnny Walker Red Label Scotch whisky and stayed during the first tumultuous months of the raucous new regime. A job was a job; in fact, it was all

Queeney had. He was not married, he lived alone in a remote neighborhood of the South Side. He was a man who led an unremarkable private life.

But his public life was far from quiet. Which made the telephone call received by a machine on a still, dark morning in Chicago not as unusual as it might have seemed at first.

The caller waited for the tone to sound and then spoke. His voice was deep, his accent was urban black:

"Acknowledge this, motherfucker. You and your trained Tom and that white fool writin' 'bout the gangs gonna die. Die, understand that? And you gonna die first you don't let up. In the name of Allah and Jesus, you have been warned and the prophecy is foretold."

That was all.

But it was the beginning of all that would follow.

__2_____

Queeney and Sweeney

Sweeney was drunk enough to know better than to return to the newsroom after a boozy lunch hour. He had been that drunk before. He once told a young reporter that "a good reporter never gets wet, always carries a roll of dimes for the phones, and never goes back to the office when he's drunk—it's a far, far better thing to hide out like a real man." Sweeney was of the old school and feigned not to take his craft seriously; the young reporter, of a new school, was very serious indeed and found Sweeney's advice distasteful.

Sweeney showed few outward signs of drunkenness as he lurched off the elevator

at the fourth floor and ambled like a large bear down the narrow corridor to the reception desk at the far end of the building. The reception desk was usually manned by a black security guard—as with other companies, most visible and unimportant positions at the newspaper were held by blacks, in deference to the minority-hiring program—and Sweeney did not know any of their names.

Francis Xavier Sweeney, fifty-three, a broad-faced, balding Irishman who wore blue dress shirts with tight collars, narrow ties, and sports jackets that were too loud and too old, pushed open the glass door at the back end of the low-ceilinged newsroom. It was Tuesday afternoon.

The large, loud room was full of desks butted together and people working shoulder to shoulder. It was noisy because it was always noisy, even in the dead time of Sunday morning when it was occupied only by the weekend overnight man.

The newspaper was in the process of installing computer terminals to replace the rickety manual typewriters, and this added to the chaos. Cables snaked across the floor, attached to cables that dangled

from panels in the false ceiling. The reporters dreaded the coming of the computers for no good reason except that it represented change. In a business concerned with reporting change and the passing of time, it was strange how conservative the participants were in such little things. So Queeney had once observed to an amused Sweeney.

Sweeney pushed down a narrow aisle between two rows of desks. Typewriters banged, the wire-service machines along the wall hiccuped the news of the world, and everywhere there was paper and grime and old newspapers. It was a perpetually dirty room inhabited by gray-faced men and women—though it was true that most of the women were actually employed around the feature-department desk in an alcove off the main newsroom. The feature section was the perpetual province of women in the business. Those on newsside called the feature section Wonderland, with obvious contempt mixed with envy at people who had more fame and regular hours on top of it.

Sweeney paused a moment while his stomach growled. He had drunk ten vodka

martinis and eaten nothing.

Shut up, he said to himself. I'll get you a hot dog later.

Sweeney was thirty pounds overweight, he had high blood pressure, his wife was a newspaper widow, and his daughter and only child had become a member of a cult in California and rarely wrote to them. Which did not matter to Sweeney. Life had become a blur to him, and he was waiting for his liver or heart to give out so that he could decently die. Death by Irish suicide, he had confided once to Queeney. "It is the only Catholic approved method of self-destruction."

Queeney.

He glanced at that moment at the glass-walled office on the window side of the room where Michael Queeney held his court.

There had been a time when he could talk to Queeney across a bar and tell him true things about drinking himself to death and about the bullshit in the newspapers and about the stupidity of his life and the cynicism that encrusted his soul like a scab that he always picked open. There had been a time.

"Friend Queeney," Sweeney said aloud as he reached his own desk and looked down at the unfinished story still rolled into his typewriter.

The goddamn story, Sweeney thought.

It had nagged him for days, it had started him on another binge of drinking his lunch and his afterwork time and fighting again with Maureen over nothing and leaving the flat in the morning sicker than he had felt the night before, always overlaid with guilt and anxiety.

The guilt, he knew, was caused by the booze.

The anxiety, he knew, was real. He had every reason to feel it.

Sweeney took off his jacket. His sleeves were rolled up and his shirt collar unbuttoned. The room was too warm in too many corners. It was winter in Chicago but a rare mild day, cloudless and clear. The January sunlight painted the buildings along the Chicago River north of the Loop in primary colors. It had not snowed for three weeks. Survival was seeming possible again. This was Chicago in the harsh winter heart of the upper Midwest and surviving winter counted as an everyday concern.

"You'll catch cold. Wearing just a sport coat to lunch."

Sweeney, staring at his typewriter, did not turn. He stared at the sheet of white paper. Fucking story and now him. He knew the voice, of course. He knew the mocking tone. He had known it since childhood. Sweeney and Queeney, the Gold Dust Twins.

"I didn't have far to go."

"I called around for you. After the first hour."

"What am I, twelve years old?"

"Sometimes."

"I had to interview somebody."

"Bullshit, Francis. Don't jack me around."

Sweeney felt the pressure building again, felt his neck seem to swell beneath the collar, felt his fingers bunch into fists resting on the keys of the elderly black Smith-Corona on the typing well of his gunmetal-gray desk.

"I wasn't in the usual places. I was talking to a guy in the Red Squad. About our friends."

"The story is buttoned up. We've been hitting it for two months. We need a couple

of more weeks of gloss on it and that's it."

Sweeney looked up, twisting his head around to see the managing editor looming over his desk. Fifty-two years old was Michael Queeney, just five pounds over the national insurance-company weight average, a guy who looked like an editor is supposed to look. Thought Francis Sweeney with contempt.

Queeney was a pale man, thoughtful behind his wire-rimmed glasses. His eyes were as bright as blue marbles. Michael Queeney had silver hair but a full head of it. He smoked a pipe, a thoughtful pipe, a new prop to complete the character. He had picked up the habit when he was lecturing at Northwestern University's Medill School of Journalism. The pipe had been the butt of Sweeney's savage humor from the first. But not to Queeney's face. Not anymore. The Gold Dust Twins from the old South Shore neighborhood had split up and gone separate ways. The parting had been inevitable and the separation was tinged with nostalgia. Queeney was a success of sorts and Sweeney was just another old hack behind the typewriter.

"I been working on the story."

"You been dick shit," said the elegant and well-mannered Michael Queeney, his voice snarling suddenly in quiet imitation of the South Side kid he once had been.

"It's—"

"It gets harder to write when you're half in the bag all the time. Come inside, Francis, I want to talk to you."

And Queeney led the way without looking back, through the tangle of desks forming a big horseshoe called the city desk, past the switchboard operated by copyboys, down the aisle formed by secretarial desks that led to the glass-walled offices. There were six offices, occupied by the publisher, the managing editor, the executive editor (who did long-range planning and rarely had part of the day-to-day operation), the city editor, and the star columnist, named Peter Markk; the sixth office was nearly always dark and shuttered. It was the preserve of John Hague, the press lord who rarely came to Chicago from his New York headquarters. Hague was the brash Canadian from Alberta province who had made all his money in oil fields and recently expanded into the newspaper publishing business; he had purchased the news-

paper the previous year.

"Close the door," Queeney said softly as he walked around his desk and sat down.

Sweeney turned and closed the door. A closed-door session, he thought. Very serious stuff. This was not about taking a long lunch hour. He thought again of his options, just as he would sometimes contemplate them while sitting in the Billy Goat tavern behind his tenth beer. He had twenty-six years on the paper, the Guild union contract provided two weeks' severance for every year if the paper was willing to say an employee was fired for "economic reasons." And Sweeney still had five weeks' vacation due. A year's pay in hand. Sweeney smiled to himself: I could take that money and go out and kill myself in a month. And not in Chicago in winter either but down on the beach at San Diego or even in Mexico, just let the booze fall down my throat until the liver turned over and died. Fuck Maureen then, fuck the kid, fuck Queeney, and fuck all.

"You're trying to throw everything away," Queeney said, lighting his pipe. Plumes of sweet smoke arose. Sweeney reached into his shirt pocket for a Salem

13

and lit it in self-defense.

"I know. My mother always said I had a bad attitude."

"We're going to win a Pulitzer prize on this story, Francis," Queeney said. "And you don't want it."

"They don't give Pulitzer prizes to guys like me," Francis X. Sweeney said.

"Not you. Us. The paper. How would it look for us, Francis, you and me, to bring a Pulitzer to Mr. Hague in his first year at the paper? None of his papers has ever won the big one before. But we're a big paper and it's our turn."

"Which shows there's still a measure of self-respect left in the world," Sweeney said. "This fucking series is bullshit, just between us, Michael. I think I've mentioned that before."

"Bullshit is in the eye of the beholder," Michael Queeney said, his face still composed.

"Two months of stories on the Brothers of Mecca, this fucked-up religion or whatever it is. And nobody gives a shit. I dream about this, you know that?"

"It shows you're getting involved in your work," Michael Queeney said.

"We write that stuff to give the suburbanites their cheap thrills. Give them their jollies like horror movies. Here are the big, bad niggers in the city, doing their ritual markings, killing chickens by biting their heads off, preaching racism and black magic and who-do-dat-voodoo-dat-dey-do so well. I could take a certain amount of it but I didn't realize this was going to be a lifetime commitment. I don't want a Pulitzer, I could use a raise."

Queeney put the pipe down. His mask of seriousness remained in place. "I did you a favor, Francis. I gave you a shot at it. For old times' sake in part, part because you're good. The best rewriteman I ever knew."

The flattery made Sweeney flush. "Michael, I am written out on the subject of the Brothers of Mecca. They are just a bunch of crazy gang members who went crazy from living in the ghetto, from being treated like niggers all their lives, who come from a long line of jive artists. . . . I mean, we're not really doing any good, we're not telling anyone something they don't know."

"Remember the death threat I got?" Queeney began.

"Yeah. And the one I got. And the one

15

Clayton got. If we all had a dime for every time somebody threatened a reporter, we'd be rich enough not to have to read newspapers anymore."

"The cops are taking it seriously enough."

"Cops take anything we tell them seriously enough," Sweeney said. "Don't start believing in this stuff yourself, Mick. You'll go over the edge."

"You're leading the way."

"Look, I am going to tell you the truth. Okay? You and me, and the door is closed. Okay?"

Queeney began to frown as Sweeney began to speak.

"Clayton is not telling the truth. That is why I am tired of this story. That is why I can't go on writing readable prose from his incomprehensible notes. I never fink on anyone. As long as the scam doesn't involve me. I'm a drunk and an asshole and all that but I don't make up things unless it's the odd quote here and there. Clayton is jiving."

Queeney did not move.

"Are you telling me that Clayton is making his story up? Is that what you're telling me, Francis?"

"I asked him stuff about that initiation

ceremony. The one that no one has ever seen before except the Brothers. About killing the chickens and the voodoo and having sex with both a Brother and a Sister . . . you know, the good stuff that got all the suburban ladies off at the kitchen table. You know, every time he talks to me about that, he's got to look at his notes."

"So what?"

"Fuck, Mick, you got your head up your ass or what? You're out there watching a ritual where people are biting chicken heads and fucking each other in the ass and you got to look at your notes to remember it? I'm half in the bag most of the time like you said, but there are a few moments in my personal history I remember with clarity, like the school fire at Our Lady of the Angels, the Grimes sisters when they were found in the forest preserve . . . you know, there are some things you are never gonna forget. And while I admit that Clayton has the street smarts you expect from someone who attended Harvard University, he isn't that unaware. I mean, he can't write but we both figure he can see. So how come he has to look at his notes every time he tells me about this

17

fucking initiation?"

"You're an asshole, you know that, Francis?" The acquired voice of the cultured managing editor dropped into the mean-streets argot they had both used as kids on the South Side. "You talk like a fucking asshole, bad-mouthing a reporter, you got no proof of nothing. I made a mistake, dealing a drunk like you in on this game. I did it for you, Francis, for old times' sake."

"Look, fuck old times. It's water down the sewer and you know it, Mick. You went up and I went down and that's the way it's gonna be. We aren't friends anymore, are we?"

"You're my friend," Michael said sadly. "A long time."

"But friendships end, Mick, you know that. I don't blame you."

"Blame me? You're the one who decided to crawl into a bottle and die," Michael Queeney said. "I am trying to save your life, asshole, I am trying to save your fucking job."

"Saint Michael," Sweeney said. "Doing this for Maureen? Think Maureen needs me in this job? Shit, the minute I die, Maureen

18

starts living again instead of being a widow. Or are you doing it for yourself, Mick?"

Michael Queeney did not speak. The color in his face was changing from a pale off-white to pink to red. Sweeney smiled. "Is it hot in the room at the top? Living with the Canuck and his band of boon-dockers? I never knew this job meant so much to you, Mick, you'd kiss any ass in the boardroom to let them keep you on. The difference between management and labor, ain't it? I'm union and I can get severance pay—"

"Listen to yourself, Francis." The voice was tight but under control. "Listen to what you're saying. You accuse Clayton of making up his investigation of Mecca, you're starting on me now. You've got problems, Francis."

"Clayton is my problem. I told him this morning."

"He told me."

"Little tattletale, eh? Well, fuck him and fuck you and fuck John Hague. Clayton is black and that's all that counts for you, all of you. He writes shit about the Brother-hood of Mecca, and in the spring the Pulitzer committee of distinguished assholes

19

will get together to give the paper the big prize for a story that's just about a bunch of fucking jives in the first place, even if it was true."

"Go home, Francis. Go home and think about things and then come back and talk to me when you're sober." The calm editor again, lighting his pipe.

"Fuck you, Mick, you forgot where you came from," said Francis X. Sweeney suddenly, slamming his fist on the desk. Michael did not move. The cold marble eyes stared at Sweeney with the indifference of the coroner's man at a homicide scene. "Remember, nobody gets pissed off like an Irishman and you have pissed me off. You and Clayton and that fucking asshole Peter Markk and his bullshit, slapping around broads, which we always fixed up with Judge Delacroix and—"

"You said more than you wanted to say," Michael Queeney said slowly. Frowning. Disapproving. As though someone had just belched at a dinner party.

"Shit," said Sweeney. He lurched up, felt blood rush to his head, felt suddenly drunk. The anger fed his thoughts but weakened his coordination. He pushed out of the glass

office, past Miss Thompson's desk, down the row of glass offices to Peter Markk's office.

The star columnist—the most quoted man in the city, according to some—was bent over his ancient Royal typewriter, slowly and surely feeding lines of copy onto a sheet of paper. He glanced up sharply at Sweeney at the door and said nothing.

"You fucking Finn," began Sweeney, the words blurry as his actions. "Who's gonna put the fix in for you the next time you do an assault on one of your groupies, you dumb son of a bitch?"

"Get the fuck out of here," said Peter Markk calmly, and he went back to the typewriter.

"You perfect asshole," said Sweeney. "I'm gonna get fired and when I do, I'm trotting off to the *Reader* and I'm gonna write the truth for a change about what a bunch of assholes work in this place, starting with the chief asshole from Helsinki which is you, you son of a bitch."

Very loudly, all of it. The newsroom suddenly became unnaturally quiet. Even the wire machines seemed to pause in mid-hiccup, humming, waiting for more news to

21

spew on the rolls of paper fed into each machine.

Michael Queeney was three steps behind the drunken reporter. He said, "Francis." Softly, almost sadly, as though calling a child home.

Miss Thompson saw it all.

Francis Sweeney turned—she would report to the other secretaries who had not been present—and he lurched toward the managing editor for a moment, and he struck Queeney across the face, knocking his glasses off. The action put Sweeney off balance, and he slammed against the glass wall and then bounced upright, alone in the narrow aisle.

Mr. Queeney, reported Miss Thompson in fascination, did not move, did not speak, did not even look for his broken eyeglasses on the floor. He merely stared at Sweeney, and Sweeney turned in that moment.

"Should I call a guard?" Miss Thompson heard herself saying.

"Just get out, Francis," said Michael Queeney very softly.

"You son of a bitch. All of you sons of bitches," said Francis Sweeney, and he made another move, and this time a burly

sportswriter who covered hockey and basketball pushed behind him and shoved him out of the narrow aisle, between the desks, toward the hallway that led to the elevators. The black security guard at the reception desk merely stared curiously at the large white man being pushed to the elevators.

Sweeney shrugged out of the sportswriter's grip at the elevators, but the writer waited until the elevator arrived. Sweeney stumbled inside and the writer pushed the "1" button. On the first floor, he walked the length of the building to the rear doors.

The brief clear January afternoon was fading. It was 4:33 and the sun was nearly down. The wind rose and the shadows loomed. Sweeney was coatless. He walked into the bar of the Corona Cafe on Rush Street three minutes after he left the newspaper building. The sun set bloodred on the low rooftops of the West Side. The long January night began before Sweeney finished his first glass of beer. By the time he had a second beer, a fellow reporter had joined him, carrying his hat and coat. Sweeney bought him a beer and started to explain his great rage and the injustices done to him, but his voice was so loud and slurred

that the bartender threw him out of the place.

It was 5:03 P.M. There was a smell of snow coming in the steady keening night wind.

It was 3:12 on Wednesday morning and Francis X. Sweeney still had not eaten. He had been drinking, save for the interlude at the paper, for fifteen hours. He was beyond drunkenness, though he was very drunk. He was viewing events in a curious slow-motion world in his mind. His eyes did not focus. He felt as though he would die if he stopped drinking.

He had left O'Rourke's Public House on North Avenue when the bar closed at 2 A.M. He had wandered down the ghetto streets south and east from the Irish pub toward Division and Wells. He was seen by at least three people.

He had found another bar but had been refused service. He had purchased a bottle of vodka instead and staggered down Wells Street to Division and then, inexplicably again, started walking west toward Cabrini-Green Homes, the black high-rise housing project that sprawled on the west end of the

Old Town neighborhood.

He broke the bottle of vodka by dropping it on the sidewalk after the first burning sip. He staggered south again, this time on Larrabee.

Francis Sweeney turned into an alley not far from the Newberry Library and Bughouse Square. He unzipped his fly and leaned against a brick wall as he splashed urine against the bricks. The urine wet his shoes and stained his trousers. When he was finished, he half-zipped his fly and began staggering east in the alley, toward the glittering remains of the old Rush Street nightclub district.

He saw the figure at the end of the alley. He stopped, thought for a moment about it, and then staggered on. Caution had long since been drowned in the night of drinking. He knew he wanted another drink. Nobody would stand in his way.

The figure at the end of the alley, shadowed by the streetlamp behind him, did not move.

Come and kill me, Sweeney said softly. Or, perhaps, said only to himself.

He saw the stump at the last moment. Not a stump but a bat. A baseball bat. A

toy baseball bat. Not a real baseball bat.

He thought about the bat.

He saw it coming and he felt lazy, floating, he knew he would not move, could not. He saw the bat swing in a wide arc toward him.

Remember the day when the Sox beat the Yankees twice at Comiskey Park? A day in summer, so warm. It was so cold now, it was always winter now. But there had been days in summer. Remember?

He smiled, and the bat smashed the side of his skull. Felt a sudden rush of loss but there was no pain. He was down, he thought, he could feel the broken cement of the alley in his hands. He was on his hands and knees.

Did not feel the second blow across his shoulders. But he was still conscious. No pain. Perhaps there was no pain. The joke was on the other guy—I'm busted, they even took away my credit card.

Felt the third blow. Pain. Very real pain.

The fourth, which broke his neck, ended the pain. He fell the little distance left to the floor of the alley, fell on his face, cutting it, his eyes wide open, strangely smiling.

_3

Why did Sid do it?

No one felt very good on Wednesday morning. The wind had picked up around six. A storm was blowing down from the Wisconsin-Minnesota border. The dawn was edgy and gray, black clouds and white pushing each other around above the grid of city streets.

Lieutenant Matt Schmidt had come in early because he had gone home early the night before. He placed his paper cup of black coffee on the desk he used, which was just inside the entrance of the little office on the sixth floor of police headquarters at 1121 South State Street.

He took off his dark-blue overcoat and

hung it on a peg he had put in the gray-green wall himself. He placed his wide-brimmed fedora on the desk and took off his blue suit jacket. He was a cadaverous man of careful, conservative dress, the old-style image of the homicide detective. In fact, that is what he was.

He turned on a single light over his desk and bathed the darkened squad room in an almost homey light. The lamp on his desk had been Karen Kovac's idea. They had all hated the glare of the coldly efficient fluorescent lighting in the room, but only Karen Kovac had suggested investing in dime-store lamps to give the room some humanity.

"A woman's touch," Sergeant Terry Flynn had teased at the time. "I like it, really; I'd like to see curtains on the windows. And plants. I'm very into macrame."

Karen Kovac had suffered the teasing in silence, and Terry Flynn had contributed his share for the three lamps. There were only two now; a week before, someone had burgled the office and taken one of the lamps. Despite a search of other divisions by Terry Flynn, it was not found. Flynn suspected Auto Theft in one of the police area headquarters had stolen the lamp.

Matt Schmidt smiled at the thought of Flynn's fruitless investigation and took the plastic lid off the coffee container. He sipped the black liquid and made a face as he always did. Gert, his wife, usually made coffee but Gert was visiting her brother in Iowa and Matt Schmidt was coffeeless in the mornings. He did not feel helpless at home—he had been a bachelor for a long time before he married—but he felt so alone without Gert in the house that all he could do was sleep there.

The electric clock on the window wall read 7:13 when Terry Flynn walked through the door. He looked tired, which he was, and hung over. He had a coffee cup as well, filled with a whitish mix of cream and coffee. He did not speak to Schmidt until he had taken his first sip.

"I feel rotten."

"You probably were the last one to leave."

"Yeah. Me and Sid. But Sid won't feel rotten. He never drinks enough to feel bad."

Schmidt tried a smile and found it fit. Terry Flynn was red-haired and blunt in features and manner. He was the son of a policeman who had been a bag man in the

29

old days. Through the grace of old connections and his father's clout, he had risen to the rank of sergeant in Homicide. No one thought he would go much further. He offended too many people who counted. He was big and muscular, though running to fat. It was commonly accepted in the squad that Terry Flynn was Karen Kovac's lover, which made his teasing less obnoxious. At least to her.

"You couldn't sleep."

"I could sleep," Terry Flynn disagreed and took another gulp of coffee. "But I felt rotten. About Sid leaving. I half figured I'd come down and there'd be Sid sitting at his desk, figuring out his expense account. I never knew a man could figure an expense account so close."

"Because he kept his receipts."

"If he'd weigh himself, he'd want a receipt from the machine," Terry Flynn said. "Jesus Christ. What the fuck is he going to do in California?"

"Not be cold," Matt Schmidt replied.

It wasn't enough. Sid Margolies had been on the department nineteen years, thirteen as a homicide detective. He had been in Matt Schmidt's Special Squad for five years.

He was a quiet, precise man with an oblique look at the world, a left-hander in a world of righties. Terry Flynn once said that if Sid described a doughnut, he'd start with the shape of the hole. It was true and apt. It was also remarkable that Terry Flynn would say such a thing.

"It isn't enough not to be cold," Terry Flynn said. "That's bullshit. I told him that. He said that wasn't it. He said he just didn't want to take it anymore. Everyone's got to eat, right? I mean, we're not young men anymore, right?" Terry Flynn seemed to be arguing with himself.

"Sid thought about it for a long time," Matt Schmidt said gently, surprised by the depth of Terry Flynn's feeling. Feeling for what? he thought: Loss of Margolies or thinking about himself in Sid's place?

A month before, Sid Margolies had decided to go on departmental leave. He said he was moving to California, he was going to find another job, he was tired of winter in Chicago, he was tired of the job. As always, his pale, thin face showed no emotion beyond the flat words. Matt Schmidt had had a long talk with him, not to change his mind but to understand why he wanted

to quit. Sid Margolies had said, finally, that in all his life, he had wanted to do something that left a small mark on the world.

"Not my ego," Sid had explained as though it were necessary. "Just do one thing or two things that made some difference. And I'm halfway to death and it hasn't been done. Maybe it's my failure; maybe it's what I chose to do. But I have to try something different."

The leave was granted; it was open-ended. Nobody expected to see Sid Margolies again. Perhaps it was the finality of that thought that moved Terry Flynn. He and Margolies had worked together for five years. They came from different backgrounds, they had different temperaments, and sometimes they did not work well together.

The going-away party, a long boozy bash at the cops' bar called O'Sullivan's on Grand and Milwaukee on the near West Side, had seemed absurd to everyone who attended. Sid Margolies was not a party cop. He seldom drank and rarely spent time after hours with other policemen. He did not live the job in that sense. He and Ruth lived in a rambling old flat in the Lincoln Park neighborhood with books and cats, an apartment

of silences in evenings spent reading. Ruth had not attended the going-away fete. No one on the Special Squad in Homicide had ever met her. She was a part of Sid's secret life that none of the rest could understand.

"You know what I think?" Terry Flynn said suddenly, lighting a Lucky Strike with a match. He blew the smoke away from Matt Schmidt but turned in his chair to face him.

"About Sid?"

"Sure. He's going to find out there isn't any place where you make your mark. Least of all California. There's just plugging away and passing time and getting laid and drunk once in a while and then you enter church for the last time with your toes turned up."

"Sid is Jewish."

"So he doesn't get a funeral mass. What difference does it make?"

Gently. "That's what he wants to find out."

Terry Flynn made a face. "People think too much about themselves."

"The unexamined life . . . ," Matt Schmidt began.

"That's crap," Terry Flynn said, finishing the Greek aphorism in his mind. "Life

is like an Italian sausage. You don't want to examine it too closely and find out what it's made out of. It might be awful stuff like pig's farts and cow dung. Just eat it and if it tastes good, count yourself lucky."

Matt Schmidt tasted his coffee again, decided he could not stand it, and dropped the cup in the metal green wastebasket beneath his desk. He rose and went to the window and stared out at the city spread beneath the violent sky. "Snow," he said.

"I smelled it coming in," Terry Flynn said. "I had the radio on, they said maybe six inches by tonight."

"Sid is taking a noon flight. I hope he makes it out of O'Hare," Schmidt said absently, filling the silence.

"I told him if he made it big out there he could adopt me. I'd be a Japanese houseboy for him, wear a rubber band over my eyelids."

"It'd be nice to be warm," Matt Schmidt said.

"When does Gert get back?"

Schmidt, his back to the beefy sergeant, grinned despite himself. Not many counted Terry Flynn very smart or very perceptive; he wore a veneer of roughness picked up

34

from his childhood on the South Side, distressed further by his years as a Tactical cop in the ghetto. But Terry Flynn understood very well about nearly everything and that is why Matt Schmidt had picked him for the Special Squad despite objections of Leonard Ranallo, the chief of Homicide, who thought Terry Flynn was merely uncouth.

The telephone rang. It was the internal department phone. Flynn reached for it across his empty desk.

"Yeah."

"This is Commander Ranallo's office. For Lieutenant Schmidt. Is he there?"

"Just a minute. I'll check the other offices." Flynn cupped the phone in his hand. Schmidt turned.

"It's Ranallo's office."

"What other offices are you going to check?" Matt Schmidt grinned. The room was office to four people and was jammed with two file cabinets, three desks, and one chair too many.

Schmidt picked up the receiver. "Lieutenant Schmidt."

"Commander wants to see you," said the secretary.

Schmidt replaced the receiver. "I'm going

35

up to see Ranallo."

"Better you than me," Flynn said.

Fifteen minutes later, Schmidt reentered the squad room on the sixth floor. Karen Kovac was at her desk, her face flushed, also drinking coffee and reading the *Tribune*. She had been at Sid's going-away party too and didn't look well.

"We have an unfortunate matter," Schmidt said. He spoke as he began pulling on his suit jacket and overcoat. Without a word, Terry Flynn got to his feet and slipped into his leather coat. Karen remained seated.

"Two beat cops in Eighteen found a body, white male, this morning in an alley off Chestnut and Dearborn. He was beaten to death with some kind of stick. Area Six Homicide handled it first. The scene is still open and everyone is standing around petrified."

"Who is he?" Terry Flynn said.

"A newspaper reporter."

"Fag?"

"It might be, it's the right area. He was pretty drunk. About fifty, maybe older. It was a very mean killing."

36

"And us?"

"You know of our commander's impressive relationship with the news media," Schmidt said. "He wants to make sure that no eggshells are cracked. He's taking it away from Area Six."

"Which makes us very popular."

"Karen. Are you still detached for that rape serial in Rogers Park?"

"Yes. But nothing's happening now. We keep going round and round. We're waiting for the next one."

"Then you'd better come along. I don't know what this is about." Matt Schmidt pulled on his hat with the wide brim. "But it doesn't smell nice."

"Like snow coming in," Terry Flynn said. And as he said it, the first flakes began to fall.

Snow carpeted the alley when they reached the North Side. Two squad cars blocked the scene, one on the street side, the other in the alley.

The body was in the middle of the alley, belly down, the face turned, eyes staring sightlessly, the mouth curved in a smile. There was blood matted in the brownish-

gray hair, blood on the side of the face, blood in a frozen pool beneath the body and extending from the neck two feet to the entrance of the alley.

Caffrey from the coroner's office was on his knees in the snow, his fingers probing gently against the rigid flesh. Caffrey was accustomed to death and more at home among the dead than the living. The smell of living men sickened him; the smell of death, cleansed by putrefaction, the silent antiseptic smells of the cutting room in the basement of the morgue on the West Side, formed the acceptable odors of his life.

Connors and Rosetti from Area Six Homicide (which covered the North Side east of the river) had been waiting.

Terry Flynn nodded to Connors and Rosetti. Everyone knew about Special Squad and everyone in Homicide resented it, even as they felt some relief when the squad was called in to handle a hot case. There were too many pressures in the city—from the machine, from the media, from other sources—when a very hot case came down; the squad was the buffer. Or the lightning rod, as Terry Flynn would say.

"Sid Margolies took off, huh?" said Connors by way of greeting. It was a truce remark and Flynn took it that way.

"Yeah. He'll be laying by the pool this afternoon when we got six inches of snow."

Snow had fallen on the body but melted into the fabric of the soiled black coat. As the policemen walked around the body or knelt next to it, they left marks on the snow.

"Who is he?"

"Francis X. Sweeney, a foin old name. Driver's license—and it's been punched a couple of times. We ran a computer check, he's had a couple of DWIs. We're looking for a car but there's nothing to match the license. Maybe his wife has it."

"Where's he live?"

"Fifty-sixth and Normandy, out by Midway Airport."

"He's a long way from home."

The last came from Matt Schmidt. He knelt down next to Caffrey.

Caffrey turned, sniffed. He had known Matt Schmidt twenty years. "He's getting hard, it was sometime in the last six hours. Drunk. You can smell him."

Schmidt touched the bloodied neck.

"Yeah," said Caffrey. "Broken. The skull caved in on this side. It's hard to tell which blow did it. Once across the back, I think; I'll know better when I strip him at the morgue."

Schmidt felt the blood on the neck and pulled his bloodied fingers back. The fragment was small, like a toothpick.

"Wood," he said.

"I figure it for something like a baseball bat or a baton," Caffrey said. Baton was the department word for nightstick. "They've been looking for something. It's round, so I'll bet on a bat. See how the skull is broken? Concave? A big stick. If it was steel, say a crowbar, it'd leave a smaller impression."

Schmidt got to his feet and brushed the snow from his knees. "You've got a baggie?"

Connors opened a plastic envelope and Schmidt deposited the sliver of wood. Then he wiped his bloodied hand on a white handkerchief.

Connors said, "We've been looking for a bat or something up and down the alley, along the side streets. Got four guys from Eighteenth Tactical out around but nobody has found nothing."

40

"He's a reporter, huh?" Flynn inter-rupted.

"Yeah," Connors said. "I knew it when I saw the press card."

"What a detective," Flynn smiled.

"We have our moments. Not downtown moves but in our own little way, we try to do our best with our limited intellects." Connors grinned back.

Rosetti opened the morning paper and showed it to the others. "He was writing stuff about the Mecca Brothers, you know, de bruthers of de new order of de mystic knights of de sea."

"Oh," said Schmidt, staring at the crum-pled hulk. "That was him. I thought it was someone black with an Irish name."

"Funny," Terry Flynn said.

"We got car keys and no car, also twelve dollars and change in his pockets and a Timex wristwatch. A bunch of pencils in the pocket of his jacket. I don't know what else."

"Just a nice random bit of street vio-lence."

"Fag," Schmidt said quietly.

Connors understood and shrugged. "You don't know. Maybe he found one of the

41

leather boys over at Bughouse Square and wanted a rough treat. But baseball bats or whatever the hell was used . . . well, it doesn't make your usual M.O. And in an alley? These guys like to have some privacy. But who knows? We just got started on this thing."

Matt Schmidt stared at Connors a moment. "This isn't our matter alone. We need some help on it." Gently, soothing away the differences.

Connors said nothing.

"Who's the third man on your team?" Schmidt said. Detective teams were three men most of the time, with a third man essentially filling in when the other two were off.

"We're all alone in the world," Connors grinned. "We had Malmon and he just got transferred out to Area Two. He likes the action better."

"We'll stay in touch," Matt Schmidt said.

Caffrey looked up from his position next to the body. "You want to close the scene?"

"You can have him," Schmidt said. "Terry. Go down to the morgue. See if you can get an accurate description of the wounds. Check out the fag thing."

"Sure," Terry Flynn said, making a face. "What about—"

But Schmidt came closer, so close that no one could hear what he said next to Flynn. His low voice was flat, cold.

"I don't want the coroner hotdogging on this. Everything comes out of the department, out of Ranallo. I don't want that bastard doing television shows on this one," Schmidt said. "Impress him. And keep the stuff quiet. And that means City News Bureau as well. At least until we can talk to the widow and the paper. This can blow right up in our face, even blow up the town. I don't like newspaper reporters getting murdered and I don't like reporters who have picked a fight with a black militant group. You see?"

"Yeah," Flynn said, making another face. It was the kind of thing he hated to be involved in. His manner was direct, his methods blunt. He was in the business of catching killers, he had once complained to Karen Kovac, not in public relations.

The scene was broken slowly, almost reluctantly. Two uniformed men from the East Chicago Avenue district station (formally, the Eighteenth District) lifted the re-

mains of Francis Xavier Sweeney and settled him in a body bag and pulled the zipper from toe to head. He was carried to a squadrol and placed inside on a stretcher. In Chicago, the police transported the dead, the fire department the living.

After ten minutes, the alley was deserted save for Karen Kovac and Matt Schmidt. None of the media had shown up, which did not displease either of them. Like all policemen, Matt Schmidt was ambivalent about the press, using it when it was docile, distrusting it when it was not.

Karen had her hands in the pockets of her gray wool coat. Her blond hair was wet with snowflakes. Her clear, cloudless blue eyes were turned to Schmidt. She had been waiting for them to be alone.

"Look at this," she said.

Schmidt stepped across the alley to a brick wall. The wall was clear of graffiti, save for one spray-painted red symbol. The symbol was complex but the spray-can artist had been patient and exact. Depicted was a triangle with an eye inside and three more eyes outside on each line of the triangle. The whole was surrounded by the depiction of a snake whose toothy jaws were opened,

nearly swallowing its own tail.

Schmidt stared at the graffiti for a moment. "What is it?"

"The Brotherhood of Mecca. The symbol."

"No one saw it," Matt Schmidt said.

"They weren't looking for it. They were looking for a weapon. It's not very old."

"No." He touched the paint. "I suppose there's some test they can do to say when it was painted."

"I don't know. Who do we tell?"

"No one, for now," Matt Schmidt said. It was too bizarre. It was too dangerous as well. "I don't like this at all."

"No." She had been the first woman in Homicide because Matthew Schmidt had picked her. She was smart and ambitious, and Schmidt did not resent that. They worked well together because Karen Kovac thought there were still things to learn from Matthew Schmidt.

"The danger is with that paper," Schmidt said. "Do you know about Jake Lingle?"

"No," she said.

Schmidt turned away from the wall, frowned, stared down the empty, depressing alleyway. Brick walls and backs of buildings

and metal fifty-five-gallon oil drums used as trash cans. What had Francis X. Sweeney thought of in his last moment on earth? What was the last thing he had seen as he fell? Nothing. Just a city alley, dark and narrow, leading nowhere.

"He was a reporter for the Chicago *Tribune* in the Capone era. He was killed by the Outfit in the Illinois Central station on Randolph Street. The *Tribune* went crazy, of course. It offered a reward, declared war on the gangs, inflamed everyone for days."

"What happened?"

"Nothing. No one ever found his killers. But they did discover that Jake Lingle had been on the payroll of Capone for years."

"What about this man?"

"Yes. What about him, Karen?" Matt Schmidt turned his mournful eyes to the place on the floor of the alley where Sweeney had fallen. It was beginning to fill in with snow. In a little while, the blood would be covered, the place of death would be returned to what it had been before, an anonymous bit of pavement in a city.

"And it might be something simple, something random, something we'll never clear," she said.

"Yes. Or something very different from what it appears. But we don't need the Hague people to fan the flames any more than they'll be fanned. I'll get someone in Evidence to take a scraping, photograph. Then I want you to get a can of spray paint, Karen. Get rid of it."

She understood. More important, she trusted Matt Schmidt's instinct.

4

The Story on Page One

"You knew him better than anyone." It was not so much a statement as an accusation and both men understood that.

Michael Queeney sat very still across the desk from John Hague. When he answered, it was in his best Sigma Delta Chi awards dinner voice: "We grew up together on the South Side. We came to the paper from City News Bureau in the same year."

"Then you write the obit."

Queeney swallowed. "It's hard. I knew him—"

"Yes, that's what'll make it better, the pathos coming through, you might say. Old boyhood chums, separated by death."

Hague spoke in a quick, clipped Canadian accent leavened by the broader vowels of the Canadian prairie. The curtains were drawn in the dimly lit office against the thin afternoon light. Queeney stared at the sallow, grinning man across from him. Did he mean anything he said? It was a question that had puzzled Queeney—and others who worked for Hague—more than once.

Queeney had called Maureen after the police contacted her to tell her of the death of her husband in an alley on the North Side in the middle of a cold January night.

It had surprised Michael Queeney that Maureen was truly grieving. He had taken one of the pool cars to the South Side to be with her until a neighbor could attend her. Maureen wept all the time Michael was with her. She wept great heaving, screaming tears that flowed out of her body like ghosts fleeing an empty house. The exorcism of the sobs shook her. Michael Queeney saw her in that moment as she had been long before, when first Michael and then Francis courted her and she favored both of them but, in the long run, chose Francis for no other reason than that she loved him. She had not loved him for a long time; but now, in the

49

sobs of that early morning, love returned.

All of which had shaken Michael Queeney as much as the death of Francis itself.

Now, in John Hague's office off the newsroom, it was nearly 4:00 P.M. The bulldog edition was already put to bed. The preparations were now being made to tear out the paper for the home edition that would find its way in the morning by ancient means to the doorsteps of 300,000 families scattered in the 262 cities, towns, and villages that formed the Chicago Metropolitan Area. By tradition, the morning newspapers in the city actually began their new cycle of publishing in late afternoon of the day before the date stamped on page one.

"The police. We consider the police," said John Hague. "This is obviously the first implementation of those death threats. The police understand that."

Michael Queeney shivered. "I don't know, I haven't talked to—"

"But we will talk to them, Queeney, and when we do, we have to make the coppers understand what this is all about, about the death threats against you and that colored fellow and Sweeney. This is all tied to the

series you were working on about the Mecca gang."

Queeney squinted. The afternoon light gave up and fell behind the buildings, succumbing to night. The owner of the paper could only be seen in dim outline. He was a small man with a rumpled white shirt and a tie loosened at the collar. John Hague, forty-seven, had inherited a failing daily in Alberta province, a radio station, and a thousand acres of mostly unusable land too far north in the province for precision farming. He was twenty-one then. When he was twenty-four, oil was discovered on the worthless land. By the time he was thirty, he owned sixty-five newspapers in Canada, Australia, and Britain. His style of journalism was blunt and tinged with a bitter edge. It was seemingly wide-eyed but was profoundly cynical. He was compared with Hearst of an earlier newspaper age. When he thought about the comparison at all—and he turned a deaf ear to most of the chorus of critics hounding him—he took it as a compliment.

He had owned the morning newspaper in the city for a year.

He had increased circulation by 20 per-

cent and cut costs drastically. The paper, once respectable, fairly liberal in tone, and fairly dull in content, certainly was not dull anymore. And no one would accuse it of being respectable either.

It was a commonplace to say no one understood this strange, sarcastic Canadian. No one understood what he wanted besides money and power. Perhaps that was it, though; perhaps it was enough. Everyone who worked for him was terribly afraid of him.

Especially Michael Queeney, the only holdover editor from the old, respectable regime.

"The police want to talk to everyone at the paper who had a connection with Sweeney on his last day. Me. And even Peter Markk. Desmond Clayton—"

"About that little display of drunkenness in the newsroom by your friend Sweeney?" The words turned like a knife. It was intended as a reprimand and Queeney took it quietly. After a moment of silence, he continued:

"Sweeney told me that he thought the story about the Mecca Brotherhood was a phony. That Clayton was making up scenar-

ios, about the initiation rites. I talked to Clayton after Sweeney left last night. We had a long talk."

"And what did Clayton say?"

"That he didn't make it up."

John Hague smiled. "Ah, I would have put money on that, wouldn't you, Michael?"

"I don't think it was made up either. Clayton compressed some scenes, disguised some identities of tipsters. He had to do that."

"Of course."

"I don't know what was eating at Sweeney."

"And our famous columnist, now what was he threatening *him* about exactly?"

"I . . ." Queeney faltered. "He alleged that a fix was made. To quiet an assault case against . . . Markk . . . that . . ."

"Come on, Queeney, give us your best journalism-school manner. Dope it out in ten seconds or less."

"We fixed a case."

John Hague smiled. "I know that, Michael. Knew it from day one. The reason I do quite well is that I know what I'm doing. More important, I know what other people are doing. You dragged your old friend

53

Sweeney into this investigation, to do the writing because Clayton can't write . . . and you did it for what reason exactly?"

"Sweeney was a good writer, one of the best."

"What reason exactly?"

Queeney waited a moment before answering. It was like first grade and Sister Mary Theresa was standing over him with an eighteen-inch wooden ruler with a metal edge and she was daring him not to finish reading the line in the "Dick and Jane" reader and he was struggling and tears were filling the seven-year-old's eyes . . . what was that word . . . pushing and pushing and finally the slap of the ruler across his fingers and in pain, he spoke the word he had known but had been unable to say a moment before.

"He was my friend."

"You jeopardized a good investigation for a bloody fucking drunkard because he was your friend," said John Hague, drawing the words out painfully.

"He performed," said Queeney, shrugging uncomfortably in his seat, seeing the rosary around Sister Mary Theresa's neck, the crucifix dangling before his seven-year-

old eyes. Did we ever escape? he thought in that moment.

"Well, he did perform at that. His finest hour was his last. A martyr to the cause of press freedom. By God, we'll goose this one for all it's worth," said John Hague. "And you're Mr. In in Chicago and you're going to put the screws on. I want nothing less than a special team investigating this murder. Police and prosecutors—what d'ya call them, state's attorney—I want everyone involved. I just ordered up an editorial to that effect. But it's up to you, Queeney, the inside man, to get it done." The voice was as cold as the place of Hague's birth. There was a brittle quality to his words—something in the timbre of his voice—that broke like icicles falling from frozen rocks.

"Bud Halligan is the state's attorney," said Queeney.

"If he wants to stay state's attorney after the next election, he better jump to the tune. And that goes for the mayor as well."

Queeney stared at Hague, a queasy feeling coating his innards. It was hopeless to explain. He had tried to tell Hague when he first came to the city that the political machine that ran Chicago did not operate—or

respond—at such a crude level in its relationships with the various news organizations. Politicians like Halligan could be intimidated on a short-term basis. But not the mayor. Not at his age, not at the height of his power. The 1970s were now half over and the mayor had been the great unchanging force in the city that swirled in change. He had been in office for nearly twenty years and had effectively destroyed any opposition to him by co-opting it. Hague, unfortunately for Queeney, believed in the power of the press. He had once helped unseat a Canadian prime minister, an easier feat than effectively threatening a mayor of Chicago.

"I talked to the chief of detectives for homicide and they've put their Special Squad on the matter," Queeney began. "I'll take up the matter with Halligan."

"Don't take it up, Queeney, tell him."

"It doesn't work that way, Mr. Hague."

"How does it work?"

"Indirectly." Queeney realized he was sweating. "You dance with these guys."

John Hague leaned forward in that moment, his face caught in the small frame of yellow light from the desk lamp. He had

very thick eyebrows and a very ordinary face. His lips were thin and his teeth were crooked. He might have been one of the people who read his newspapers and played his lottery games, who lived on a diet of hope and scandalous headlines and who dreamed at night they would someday win enough money to buy a new car.

"I'm not going to bite you, Queeney," said John Hague with a smile. "I do appreciate your skills. You know this city. It's a baffling sort of place, isn't it? But I want pressure put on, I want it so hot that they find the killers of Sweeney in hours, not days. I want a bombardment."

"There is some danger—"

"Death threats. To you and Clayton and Sweeney, serious enough to tell the police about. This is about our investigation into the Brothers of Mecca and we're not going to be intimidated. Period."

"There is still some danger," Queeney continued.

"Racial? You mean the coloreds might riot because you put the heat on? See, that's it. You Americans always tiptoe around saying the obvious, really you do. This is anarchy, man, tearing this country apart, one

rule for blacks and one for whites. You can't have two nations in one or you end up with no nation at all. Like we have in Canada with the bloody Separatists in Quebec. Anarchy, crime, bombs. Well, you don't put up with it. Not if you're white or colored. You say, 'Enough of the gangs and crime in the streets and enough of terrorists and drug pushers and all the rest of them.' That's what you say and you say it in the name of liberty or civil rights or whatever." The voice was still brittle, still cool, chattering like the disinterested rattle of a lone machine gun firing at the end of a war.

Queeney said nothing.

"We take care of our own, our fallen comrade, we are going to make Sweeney's death just what it really was—a cause, like that fellow in Arizona took on the mob and got killed for it."

Hague leaned back, away from the light again. The interview was over. Queeney rose.

Hague said, "I'll supervise the page make-up tonight. I want this splashed big. I'm going to stay over in Chicago for a few days—" He pronounced the name of the city wrong and Queeney winced. "I'm going

to be right on top of this matter."

Queeney returned to his own glass-walled office and sat down behind his desk and pulled a typewriter on a portable stand toward him. He slipped a piece of paper in the machine and turned the platen.

"SUB SWEENEY OBIT" he typed in the upper left hand corner.

At that moment, Peter Markk stood in the door. Queeney glanced up, annoyed.

"We're gonna make the asshole a saint now, right?" said Peter Markk in his gravelly, sneering voice. He was smiling sardonically, a cigarette fastened to his thin lips.

"Yes," said Michael Queeney because he was too tired tonight to fight any further with anyone.

"I suppose the Canuck wants to burn down the ghetto to find the killer, right?"

"Not exactly."

"Maybe we could have a lottery game to pick the hour and day the arrest is made," said Peter Markk. "I think Sweeney made a wise career change by getting killed."

Queeney suddenly felt as though he were inside Sweeney's dead body, being insulted by the columnist whose jibes were famous in the city and across the country. It was

not the first time in the past twelve hours he had felt inside Sweeney, as though clearly seeing the hopeless world he left, though he was dead and his eyes were sewn shut by the undertaker.

"Sweeney was my friend, Peter."

"Well, he's safer now than when he was alive."

"Safer?"

"A good reporter knows when to keep his mouth shut," said Peter Markk. "Now he doesn't have to worry any more about saying too much."

_____5_____

The Squeeze and the Suspect

Thomas J. (Bud) Halligan felt ill. But he could not stop reading the editorial on page two over and over as his driver, Jackie Nells, pushed the gray Oldsmobile down the clotted length of the Kennedy Expressway, toward the gloomy towers of the Loop.

On a normal morning, Halligan would peruse the papers amiably in the front passenger seat, oblivious to Jackie's erratic driving. Jackie had been with him a long time as coat-holder, morale-booster, and campaign gofer. Jackie was not much good at anything, but he did everything with a touching loyalty for the state's attorney. As Halligan's coat-holder, he was on the payroll

of the state's attorney's office with the official title of "special investigator" at $26,500 a year. It was the least Halligan could do for him.

"I don't see how they can go after you like that, the paper supported you in the last election," Jackie Nells said compassionately, glancing from the stacks of cars ahead of him to the boss.

"That was the last election," Bud Halligan said. He was a heavyset, amiable party hack who had surprised everyone by winning the machine's nomination to the sensitive post of state's attorney. Hardly anyone outside the office credited him with understanding it; insiders knew that it was Halligan's gray eminence who had cut the deal with the machine bosses for the nomination and who actually ran the office as First Assistant. His name was Leland Horowitz, he had been brought into the machine in the days of Jake Arvey, and he understood the politics of the office, even if Halligan did not. Halligan was a buffoon but a congenial one.

Which was why he was so hurt and upset by the bad things that had been said about him in the special editorial on page two by John Hague's newspaper this morning.

"Didn't we play ball with them?" Jackie said. "Didn't we go out of our way to indict one of those Mecca guys and cut no deal? We been good with those guys and then they do this to us." Jackie was taking it personally, as he did all attacks upon the boss. "You know, I know newspaper guys for forty years. I been around them, I even bought them drinks. You know what they are? Bums. When it comes down to it, they got no loyalty, they got no conscience. I could be drinking all night with one of those guys in the days when I was drinking, and you know what? They never buy a drink. They put a dollar on the bar and it gets lonely sitting there all night."

Halligan barely heard him. He was thinking about the pain in his belly and the certain knowledge that Leland Horowitz would be waiting for him in the second-floor offices in the Civic Center building. He wondered sometimes if he was afraid of Lee.

Jackie pulled off the expressway at Washington Boulevard and crawled east into the Loop. Yesterday's snow had not lived up to expectations. Only four inches had fallen but it was enough to clot the arteries for the morning rush-hour traffic.

The streets were damp and slick with ice. The wind was brutal. Men and women bent like stoop laborers into the wind as they edged along the snow-clogged walkways. The buildings formed ominous, gray canyons. Everything about the day and the effect of the weak light on the cold buildings made Halligan feel sicker.

Jackie guided the Olds into the underground parking garage beneath the rusty exterior of the Civic Center, a skyscraper on a broad square across Clark Street from the City Hall and County Building. In five minutes, Halligan slipped into the back door of his maze of offices on the second floor of the building. This was usually safety and refuge because it housed the civil division of the prosecutor's staff. The alien, even exotic criminal division was safely buried on the far West Side at Twenty-sixth and California. Halligan rarely visited criminal court except to hold a press conference.

Lee Horowitz was waiting.

Neither man said a word as Halligan took off his cashmere tan overcoat and hung it on a hanger in the closet of his office.

Lee seemed very calm. He was a small man in his early sixties with steel-gray hair

and intense blue eyes. Because he said nothing, Halligan felt all the worse.

Halligan closed the closet door at last—he had taken his time, the way a child will stall the inevitable—and stared at his First Assistant.

"So what do we do?" Halligan said.

"Remember the business with that kraut on the Northwest Side was killing all those women?"

"Yeah," said Bud Halligan. He did not sit down. It was absurd: he was the boss, Lee Horowitz merely his campaign manager and adviser and the number-two in the office, but Lee's stance did not invite Halligan to sit down.

Lee continued in a dreamy soft voice, unlike his normal snarl:

"I was thinking about that when I read the editorial this morning. This is just as bad as that was."

"It's worse. For us. It's lousy, it stinks," said Halligan. "These guys got no loyalty. Fucking newspapers."

"Yeah. Remember when they wanted an indictment last year against the alderman, came to us with that bullshit evidence. The problem with those guys is they start off by

writing stories but then when they read the stories they invented in their own papers, they think the stories get truer because they're in print. Reporters I know spend their lives bullshitting themselves and trying to bullshit you."

"But why did they do this to us?" Halligan almost whined. "We're open to them, a lot more than a lot of people have been in this office."

"If you're open to a reporter, he thinks you're a whore, the neighborhood punchboard. Bud, this is a shot across the bow of the boat, you might say," Horowitz continued. "They want to get our attention. So they got it. I called up that schmuck at the paper, Mike Queeney, the managing editor."

"What did he say?"

"He said we should talk. He said John Hague wanted him to let us know that he wasn't real happy the way we're prosecuting the Mecca schwartzers, he says he wants to see more progress on the tax indictment. Not to mention they're pissed off about this Feeney guy that got killed."

"Sweeney."

"Whatever."

"So what do we do?"

"We come down with the indictments this afternoon on the tax thing against the Mecca assholes. But that's not what this is about. You know what this is about?"

Halligan stared.

"This is about the kraut on the Northwest Side a couple of years ago."

"It is?"

Now Lee Horowitz started moving around the large, carpeted room, waving his arms, talking aloud but really talking to himself, pursuing thoughts that were tumbling down a hill too fast for words to catch.

"This is about putting together a Special Squad between us and the cops like we did then, get the heat off us, share it with the cops. We put Jack Donovan on it just like we did before, we got the same cast at the police department, we have a joint press conference, we announce that no stone will be unturned until we find the man who killed What's-His-Name and until we have discovered everything about this gang."

"The Mecca Brotherhood?"

"Brothers of Mecca," corrected Horowitz. "You see, we get the cops in on it, let them get messed up with it the same as we are.

The Brothers own thirty-five buildings they haven't paid taxes on, they claim they're a religion, nobody wants to really touch it. So we touch it. We make them the outlaws."

"What has this got to do with Sweeney?"

"Everything, Bud. We are on a holy crusade to find the killer or killers and blah-blah-blah. Shove the blame off right away on this gang and stand back. Look, a newspaper's gotta have a villain. They're just testing their guns, shooting at us. Give 'em the shines."

"But what about the . . . the blacks?"

"Voting, you mean? Look, Bud, you got a problem. You gotta make a choice. You want the blacks, you want John Hague on your neck next spring? The blacks are always gonna stay in line anyway, right? I mean, they gonna vote for a Republican, for Christ's sake? We got the organization behind us, Bud, but they ain't gonna stay behind us if those cocksuckers at the papers start shooting at us. The Man on Five doesn't need that kind of shit."

The reference to the mayor, who was the boss of the machine, put the matter in a different light for Halligan. Last week, sitting in the Walnut Room restaurant at the

Bismarck Hotel where all the politicians ate lunch, he had waved at the mayor from his table. The mayor had ignored the wave. Jackie Nells said the mayor hadn't seen him and Halligan had believed it. Until now. Maybe the mayor had someone else in mind for the job. Maybe the mayor didn't think Bud Halligan was the man to be state's attorney.

"What do I have to do, Lee?"

"I'll take care of it," Lee Horowitz said. "I already talked to our friend at the mayor's office. He likes the idea, he's gonna impress it on the department, we'll coordinate the conference for late afternoon so we hit the TV but make the *Daily News* and *Today* blow their last deadline. After all, Hague runs a morning newspaper, he doesn't want to read about it before he prints it."

"But what are we going to announce exactly?"

"That we are prosecuting this Jesus Mohammed and his gang for failure to pay taxes, for operating slum housing, for anything we can find in the civil statutes. For starters. Then we also announce the joint police investigation . . . a Special Squad

. . . blah-blah-blah. I put Jack Donovan in charge, you know, all the shit about the resources of the department and this office devoted to finding the killer or killers of Sweeney. We also announce we'll coordinate with the FBI on this, that ought to surprise those assholes at the Federal Building. We're going to bury this thing so much that nobody is going to find out what's going on, by which time, if we get lucky like we did last time, everyone either forgets about it or the cops stumble across whoever did it. The thing, Bud, is to show the newspapers that we're working on it. And you gotta start that with a press conference."

And Halligan suddenly understood and, for the first time that morning, managed to see the brighter side.

6

Leave It to Donovan

Jack Donovan locked the door of his office and walked to the tall window that overlooked an air shaft in the cramped, dirty quarters of the state's attorney's criminal division. The offices were housed in a rabbit warren of small rooms and clogged corridors full of files of dead cases that straggled along one side of the second floor of the Criminal Courts Building at Twenty-Sixth and California. The building was gray, like the day and the slum neighborhood around it. The building presented a classic front of pillars supporting a roof line and tall, gloomy windows. Behind the façade of the Criminal Courts Building was the sprawling, vastly

more ugly complex of the Cook County Jail where thousands of men served sentences or merely were held without bond awaiting trial for weeks and months. The two buildings were tied by a courtyard full of squadrols and sheriff's prisoner-transport vans as well as a tunnel that brought prisoners to cages in the Courts Building where they awaited trial.

But the window in Jack Donovan's office was blind to this vision. It was only a dirty air shaft that trickled thin winter light against the streaked windows. He was the chief of the criminal division, a tired, thin man of perpetual indecision who, somehow, managed to keep the machinery from rattling too much or stopping altogether. He had once been a cop and he had gone to night school to become a lawyer. In the process he lost his wife and his hope of ever understanding the system. Donovan half-sat, half-leaned against the window ledge with his back to the window and looked at the large man sprawled on the leather couch.

"I want to quit," Jack Donovan said. "This is really too much. Not this time. This is too dirty. I know everything Lee Horowitz wants to do."

"You mean he's finally broken the Irish camel's back?" Mario DeVito grinned up at Donovan. His belly spilled over his trousers and strained the small buttons of his white shirt. The shirt itself, fresh in the morning, had turned gray by early afternoon. The old building was full of dirt, full of unwashed grit, full of strange odors of sweat and urine and even blood. It was as frightening to some as the jail behind it, but Mario DeVito had grown accustomed to the grime and the smells in nine years as a prosecutor.

Jack Donovan was not Mario's only friend; but, in a curious way, Jack Donovan probably considered Mario DeVito his only friend. They had started about the same time in the SAO. Donovan, for no particular reason, had been named chief of the division and Mario had been named his deputy. Both men knew it could have been the other way around. Both men understood that Jack Donovan needed Mario more than Mario needed him.

"The matter of prosecuting the Brotherhood of Mecca for slum ownership and nonpayment of property taxes is for the civil division. It's a clear-cut matter. But Lee wants to muddy the waters."

73

"A newspaper guy gets killed, it tends to upset people like Lee. Especially when bricks get thrown at Uncle Bud," Mario said happily. In a pleasant way, Mario reveled in the anarchy of the moment, just as he enjoyed the stinging, day-to-day battles in the criminal courts. Jack Donovan thought Mario should have been division chief. Jack Donovan thought that he was only getting older and a little more worn down each day, while Mario seemed to get stronger.

"The cops won't like this arrangement. Hell, I don't like it. What can I do except get in their way?"

"This is a very political case, Jackie boy, in case you didn't notice it. Lee wants you to carry the ball downtown for the Gipper and if some justice accidentally gets done, well, all the better."

Jack Donovan was forty-two. He had red hair that was receding and green eyes. He never ate very well and he was too thin. He sometimes thought he had a stomach ulcer but he did nothing about it. He did nothing about a lot of things. His indecision might have been the sign of character weakness; in fact, it stemmed from Jack Donovan's hor-

rible clarity of vision, of seeing all actions shaded in gray, some darker gray than others, but all confused between what should be done and could be. He had been a policeman once. He had had a wife once. He had been a lot of things once. Now he didn't know what he had become.

"I told him I wouldn't do it," Jack Donovan said.

"Well, fine, Jack. Your problem is solved. You won't do it."

"Mario. Cut it out."

"You want to do it, you mean? Then do it. What's the worst thing could happen to you if you didn't go along with Lee?"

"I'd get fired."

"So what? This is America and you're a lawyer. You ever hear of a poor lawyer except for some noble Mickey the Mope who wants to do good in the world and wears blue jeans to court? This is Chicago, Jack. The only difference would be you'd be getting paid to defend these scum instead of putting their ass in jail. You do your act, wash your hands after conferring with them, don't sit on any strange toilet seats, and go home at four o'clock every afternoon. In a year, you'd own a Cadillac and in two years,

you'd have a Mercedes. Believe me, Jack, it gets real hard to work up sympathy for you."

Jack Donovan said nothing for a moment. His thin lips finally framed a reluctant smile. "You are a prick, Mario."

"Listen, Jack, you want a heart-to-heart, go write a letter to Ann Landers. You want someone to tell you everything is gonna be all right, find a priest, they'll tell you anything you wanta hear. Better yet, get a court-appointed shrink to hold your hand, he'll tell you that apples are brown if you want to hear that. But you talk to me, you gotta give me something better than crybaby stuff about quitting."

"This isn't what this is supposed to be about," Jack Donovan said quietly, and it surprised Mario DeVito because Jack meant it. He sat up on the couch and stared across the gloomy room at the thin man at the window.

"Jack, you're too old to believe in miracles and too long a lawyer to believe in justice. What do you think this is all about, anyway? It's us against them. We're on the side of the Medicis against the barbarians in Genoa; we get paid for it."

"The problem is Marcus Elijah."

Mario DeVito had known that since Jack invited him into the office. He had waited for Jack to bring it up.

Marcus Elijah had spent the past six weeks in County Jail, awaiting trial on armed-robbery charges. He had been a factotum in the strange, semireligious cult called the Brothers of Mecca formed two years before in the South Side ghetto from the remnants of an old black street gang. There was no doubt in Jack Donovan's mind that Marcus Elijah was being framed on the armed-robbery charges. Even that he was an accomplice to the frame.

"Yes," Mario DeVito said. "I wondered when you were going to get around to it."

"I think we were getting ready to cut a deal with Murphy." Alec Murphy was the court-appointed defender for Elijah. He had dug up the inconsistencies in the evidence and convinced Jack Donovan that Elijah was—as he had insisted from the beginning—not guilty of the brutal holdup of Pap's Liquors on East 47th Street on a night in September. Murphy had talked privately with Donovan about his "discoveries," and both of them had agreed to let Marcus Elijah

go, to quash the indictment and do it quietly.

"So cut a deal," Mario said. "As the Gipper says, 'Justice delayed is justice denied.' "

"Uncle Bud has changed his mind. Now he wants us to press for trial. He forgot everything I told him. They can't afford to ease up on anyone connected with the Brothers of Mecca."

"He told you that?"

"Lee Horowitz told me that. It's the same thing," Jack Donovan said in the same quiet voice. The room was as still as the winter day beyond the window. Late afternoon in Criminal Courts, after the trials are recessed, the prisoners returned to their cells, the judges all home, and the lawyers all refighting old cases in Jean's Bar down the street: all is quiet, unfinished, unsettled.

"That sucks, Jack," Mario said finally. "Lee Horowitz won't be in court holding a bag of shit. I'm not going to prosecute ole Marcus when it turns out half the population of Louisville, Kentucky, saw him at his mama's funeral the day he was supposed to be robbing Pap's."

78

"One little victim in the machinery of justice."

"The problem with Marcus Elijah is that he's such a rotten example of an innocent victim," Mario DeVito replied. "Rapist, did eight years in Marion, now he's a terrorist for that bunch of druggists called the Mecca Boys. If he only had a sainted mother scrubbing floors or something, it'd be easier to work up the juices for him."

"Someone set him up on this one. The cops, the gang, someone. He's the wrong man."

"So let him go."

"I got the grand jury to indict in the first place."

"Grand juries can be wrong. In fact, it's amazing to believe that occasionally grand juries can be right."

"They do what we tell them," Jack Donovan said.

"Like good little citizens."

"If I let Marcus go, Hague's sheet goes after me—"

"They're newspaper men, Jack. They don't carry guns."

"Or go after Bud, which puts Lee on my case."

Winter afternoon began shades of gloom beyond the window; night was coming early. Jack Donovan stood up and turned at the window, stared at the emptiness of the air shaft as though he were seeing something.

"How's your kid?" Mario DeVito said.

"She's fine. She wants to be a lawyer now."

"She'll outgrow it. Bring her down here in summer, let her see how justice gets done."

"Baptism by fire." He smiled fondly in the window glass. "She'd love it, I'm afraid."

"Idealism is perfidious," Mario DeVito said.

Kathleen was fifteen, very precocious. The night Rita ran away from her father's house, where she and the two children had lived since the separation, Jack Donovan was forced to become a parent. The boy had stayed there with the old man in the old house in the old South Side neighborhood. But Kathleen had come to live with Jack. Three years before. No one had seen Jack Donovan's wife since; her name and description in the FBI bulletin were on yellowing paper in half a thousand police-

department offices throughout the sprawling country. Was she dead? Sometimes, awake at dawn, Jack Donovan would lie in bed, trying to remember little Rita O'Connor next to him in the first year they were married, her body curved against him, her breath like milk. He would remember little things but he could not remember her as she had been, all of her presence.

"So what are you going to do, Jack?"

Maybe he had known from the moment Lee Horowitz called him. He walked to the desk and picked up the phone and dialed the internal number for Lee's office downtown in the Civic Center.

He said his name and waited. Then: "Lee? Yeah. Okay, Lee. Yeah. Okay. Okay. Sure, I'll be there. When's the press conference? Okay. I'll be down there, I want to talk to Matt Schmidt after it's over. . . . What? Well, I changed my mind, I guess. Yes. Yes. Okay. . . ."

Mario was silent on the couch, watching Donovan with heavy-lidded eyes and a flicker of amusement at the corners of his mouth.

Jack Donovan stared across at him. His eyes were bland. "Can you get Alec Murphy

this afternoon? Judge Longo is still in the building."

"I suppose."

"Let's set up a time," Jack Donovan said.

"Tomorrow morning early enough?"

"Not for Marcus Elijah, but it'll have to do. Tomorrow morning, early, before the reporters get in. I want to give Uncle Bud a day or two of breathing room. And Matt Schmidt, for that matter."

Mario grinned. "The shit'll hit the prop wash when they find out you let a Brother go."

"Well, the main thing is to keep the lid on Alec Murphy for a day or two, stop him from crowing about it. And if I don't move now, Alec'll go to the *Sun-Times* and spill that he found the guy was innocent but we were keeping him in jail. It's always the papers, isn't it? It'll come out eventually."

"But Lee will have to take the heat because you'll be anointed as head of the special investigative team looking into the murder of Francis X. Sweeney. So he's not going to bad-mouth you right after naming you as the big cheese of the big special investigative team."

Donovan smiled, for the first time that

afternoon. His stomach didn't feel as bad as it had earlier. "Lee put me in a bad situation," Jack said.

"So he deserves what's coming to him," Mario DeVito grinned.

Jack Donovan nodded. "Something like that."

7

Inside the Brothers

Desmond Clayton sat in the straight-backed folding chair at the end of the table. He had a notebook in front of him, as well as clippings arrayed on the table. Next to him was an attorney named Frank Coldwell who earned $500 an hour when the newspaper used him in situations like this. Which is to say, when he was protecting his client from police harassment.

Terry Flynn stared at the reporter for a long moment before resuming. The room was windowless, like a police interrogation room, but there was no ability to work up a sense of dread of authority that could be used in a police room. This was an office in

Hague's newspaper building; this was Desmond Clayton's turf and Sergeant Flynn felt frustrated by that fact.

Flynn still wore a sheepskin coat that had seen better winters. It was dirty and he had meant to get it cleaned all summer and now it was too late. It was open to reveal Terry's white shirt and tie. All homicide detectives, under directive of Commander Ranallo, dressed "appropriately" on the job. As Ranallo had put it, "I don't want my dicks looking like those cowboys in robbery with forty-eight pistols strapped to their ass like fucking Wyatt Earps." Or words to that effect.

"How long were you . . . part of the Brothers?"

"Three months."

"You see any action?"

Frank Coldwell rested his hand on Desmond Clayton's sleeve. "You don't have to answer that question. I would advise you not to. Your answers are contained in the articles printed in the newspaper and any further attempt to elicit information is for the purpose of self-incrimination."

Terry Flynn closed his eyes for a moment. Coldwell had interrupted six times in

a half hour with similar advice. Flynn doubled his fists, opened his eyes, even counted to ten like a cartoon character. It never worked. He knew his face was flushed and he felt dangerous.

"Look, Desmond, I'm not trying to incriminate anybody except the person or persons who killed Francis Sweeney in an alley."

"We appreciate that, sergeant," Frank Coldwell said in his best rumbling, summation-to-the-jury voice. He wore a three-piece suit as though born to it. He was not an old man—just past forty—but he had the bearing of a dignified old man. He could have been a judge if he had wanted to take a cut in pay.

"Sergeant," Desmond Clayton began in a curiously high-pitched voice. "I'm trying to cooperate." His tone was patient, as though suffering at least one and possibly two fools in the same room. "If I knew anything to find the people who killed Frank, I'd do it. We worked together."

"He wrote your stories?"

Desmond Clayton winced. "He was senior rewrite, he helped polish them, develop them. . . ."

"Did you write the stories?"

"I was the reporter and—"

"Look, I am trying to understand why someone went after Sweeney. He didn't know the gang he was writing about—"

"They're more complicated than that."

Terry Flynn looked surprised. "Than what?"

"Than to call them a gang. It's not a gang. If you read my stories—"

"I read them," Terry Flynn said. "I also talked to Narcotics and Gang Crime. The Brothers of Mecca is the remnants of the old Black Apostles street gang that was running most of the dope in Area Two. As far as we know, they're still running it, parts of it anyway, under this religious cover . . . that's why they own all those buildings and don't pay taxes on them. Just like the Catholic Church."

Desmond Clayton began again as though speaking to a retarded child. "The police version of facts is not the only version."

"It's the only version I'm interested in right now," Terry Flynn said, the hostility creeping up again. God, he thought, he didn't like reporters at all. Even less than lawyers. "Why are we dancing?"

Desmond Clayton blinked. So did Frank Coldwell.

"All I want is to find the people who killed Francis Sweeney, okay? Let's start from square one. Give me some ideas about the kind of people you ran across under cover, give me some idea of who might want to blow away a reporter."

"I don't—"

But Flynn interrupted. "Desmond, you see this lawyer sitting next to you? You paying him? This lawyer is the lawyer for the paper, not for you."

"Mr. Clayton is amply protected by the newspaper—"

"I'm getting tired of this, you know?" Terry Flynn realized everything he was saying was wrong, that everything he said would get him into serious trouble. This matter was too hot for someone with Terry Flynn's temperament. So he had told Matt Schmidt earlier in the afternoon, before the press conference announcing the formation of a special investigative unit.

"My client has a right to remain silent," Frank Coldwell said. "You are treating him like a suspect."

"I'm treating him like I treat everyone," Terry Flynn said.

"You mean, sergeant, the way you treat black people," Desmond Clayton said.

Terry Flynn stared at him again for a long, silent moment. He tried a guess then, twisting away from the net that Clayton and Coldwell had thrown over him. "Who threatened you?"

Yes, he thought suddenly. For a moment, Clayton's eyes widened, remembering something. For a moment, there was fear in the stuffy, windowless room, fear of something beyond this place.

"Why'd you ask that?"

"Because I'm a good guesser."

"Nobody—"

"Don't bullshit me, Clayton."

Coldwell interrupted: "I object to your unfortunate rhetoric."

"Good," said Terry Flynn, still fixing Clayton with his hard eyes. "Who was it?"

"Jesus Mohammed," Clayton said.

"How'd he get to you?"

Softly. "On the street outside my apartment. In Hyde Park."

"What'd he say?"

"You don't have to answer—"

"Shut up, Mr. Coldwell. What'd he say?"

The breakdown was sudden, total. Clayton was not in this room; he was on the street outside his apartment building in Hyde Park on a winter-hard day, beneath bare trees. Waiting and listening.

"He said, 'Nigger, why'd you do it to me?'"

Terry Flynn waited. He barely breathed. Even Frank Coldwell seemed transfixed by the softness of Clayton's voice, a voice from a dream.

" 'You know you're dead, nigger. You know it. You betrayed the people. The Brothers.' I didn't say anything. I walked into the building. I had my key out. He was standing there, on the sidewalk. He must have come out of the gangway next to the building. He was waiting for me, I don't know how long he was waiting. He just stood there, watching me. I was nervous. Hell. I was scared. I had my key out and I couldn't get it in the lock. It was like a dream. I was pushing on the door and it wasn't opening. I turned around, see if he was behind me. But he was just standing there, smiling sort of sad, you know, just standing there looking at me."

"You call the cops?"

"No."

"You tell anyone?"

"I told . . . Sweeney."

"What'd Sweeney say?"

"He said it was all 'colored mumbo jumbo'."

Terry Flynn watched Clayton's face. The reporter's large eyes were wet now. "Sweeney. Man, I never thought no one go after that old man. That old man."

"How come you didn't tell anyone else?"

"I thought . . . I thought it'd blow away."

"You should have told someone," Terry Flynn said.

"Is that right?" The wetness was still there in the eyes but they had turned hard, black almonds burning. "Where do you live, sergeant? You tell me?"

"In the city."

"Out there on the South Side or on the Northwest Side, you're surrounded by your own kind, cops, firemen. You know where I live. I'm in Hyde Park. Integrated. I'm an upper-class black dude, you know. You think you ever can escape people like Mohammed? Not with this color skin, you

can't." The soft voice was urgent now, lower in registry. "I saw you the minute you walked in here, you're another Irish cop, gonna break down the nigger, find out if the nigger's protecting some other nigger that killed that old man. That's the way that old man was too. He taught me a lot. Not about writing. He taught me a lot about me still being a nigger. To him. To you. I went to Harvard. My father was at the United Nations. You even know that? I've lived in this city three years and I know what I am. Between you and Sweeney on one side and people like Jesus Mohammed on the other. You think I'm gonna call the police because a nigger threatens another nigger?" Clayton had used the epithet each time slowly and provocatively and with a cry of pain in his voice, as though by repeating the hated word, he might exorcise it from his soul. He closed his eyes a moment and then opened them and stared at his hands resting on the table in front of him. "If I get out of Chicago in one piece," he said, very softly, "I'm never coming back."

Terry Flynn nodded. "I understand."

"You don't understand nothing," Clayton said.

"No, maybe not. I only think I do. That's all for now," he said, rising. "Now I want to talk to Mr. Queeney."

8

The Unholy Martyr

Terry Flynn did not like it. He'd intended to talk to Peter Markk separately, but the columnist was in Michael Queeney's office when Flynn entered with the lawyer, Coldwell, in tow.

"This is a convention?" said Peter Markk, guffawing quickly at what he considered his jest.

Flynn stared from him to Queeney to Coldwell. "I want to talk to you separately," he said in the cold cop's voice that implied nothing.

"Why? Don't you think we'd get our stories straight?" said Peter Markk.

"This isn't a movie and you're not a sus-

94

pect," said Terry Flynn.

"Coldwell? You can leave us alone."

"But Michael—"

"It's all right, Frank. I want to tell Sergeant Flynn something."

The lawyer reluctantly closed the door. For a moment, both Markk and Flynn stared at Queeney.

Michael Queeney looked bone tired. He had spent half a night with Maureen. He had sent out messages to the California Highway Patrol to search for Francis Sweeney's daughter among the cultists living on a ranch near Modesto. He had not permitted himself the luxury of a drink since the ordeal began. He felt used up.

"Sweeney was drunk on the last day of his life," Queeney began, and Peter Markk stared at him in something like quiet horror. What was he going to tell the cop?

"He told me he thought the story on the Mecca Brotherhood was being faked. I'm telling you this in confidence, which I hope you can respect. Because I subsequently investigated and I am convinced the story is true in all details."

Sergeant Terry Flynn had not expected this. He had been prepared for lies.

"He was unhappy with the story, with the death threats made against him, with work in general . . . a sort of malaise. Francis had become an alcoholic—"

"He probably was an alcoholic from the minute he found out as an altar boy where the priest puts the sacramental wine after mass," said Peter Markk. Queeney glanced at him sharply. Peter Markk could say anything he liked because he was the most powerful employee of the paper. Including Michael Queeney or the executive editor above him. Even John Hague had made an effort to be cordial to Peter Markk when he bought the paper and began his wholesale changes.

"Go ahead," said Sergeant Flynn, ignoring the columnist who lounged in a large leather chair to the side of the desk. "What else was on his mind?"

"I don't know. We'd been friends since we were kids. But not the last few years. It happens. I turned out to be Sweeney's boss and Sweeney was always the kid on the railroad tracks, throwing stones at the trains passing by. You know."

Flynn nodded. He knew.

"I want to be careful, to tell you only

what happened, to separate my feelings from what was actually said. You understand?"

Terry Flynn said nothing. His face did not change expression.

"I told him he was on thin ice, or words to that effect. We both knew it. He was forcing me to fire him, you see. He couldn't walk away himself, I think. He wanted me to end it for him." Queeney's eyes were wet and the cold, marble blue had become not so clear.

"He rammed out of the office and went down to threaten Peter Markk in his office. We were all there, there must have been a dozen witnesses. He brought up something that happened a half-dozen years ago."

"Fuck you, Queeney," said Peter Markk, his color rising. "Shut the fuck up."

Queeney stared at the columnist. Queeney's eyes were dull pools in a deep forest, clouded and still. "This is the police, this is a murder, Peter. This is not a game."

Terry Flynn felt the tension in the room.

"A half dozen years ago, Peter became involved with a woman. It doesn't matter who she is. One of the newspaper groupies that hang around Riccardo's on Friday nights. Young."

"She wanted to suck my column," said Peter Markk. "You'd be surprised how many broads want to do that."

"Yes," said Terry Flynn, turning slightly, his face still impassive, trying to sort the jumble of words and thoughts and images that were tumbling in his head. "I would be surprised."

Peter Markk flushed dangerously.

Queeney said, "She threatened Peter with sexual assault charges."

"It's simple. I took her to my place and slapped her around a little. She liked it. She liked everything I was doing to her. She was a goof."

"What happened?" said Terry Flynn.

"Nothing happened," said Peter Markk. "The case wasn't prosecuted."

"We helped," said Michael Queeney. "We talked to some people on the police. . . . People that Sweeney knew. Sweeney fixed it. They told the young woman she didn't stand a chance. We took care of her hospital bills and—"

"What are you telling me?" began Terry Flynn, who was taking a dislike to both of them. "She ended up in a hospital? That's slapping someone around?"

"A contusion of the eye. It turned out not to be important," said Michael Queeney, his head down now, his hands pressing together. "It probably wasn't the way to handle it. It was a long time ago."

"Six years ago."

Terry Flynn said, "Who fixed it?"

"I don't think that's relevant."

"I don't want to step in minefields," said Flynn.

"No," agreed Michael Queeney. "I suppose you don't. But it can't leave this room."

"You think I want to tell the fucking department about it?" Terry Flynn bristled.

"Yeah," said Peter Markk. "A cop's got to watch his own ass in something like this, doesn't he?"

Flynn glared at him then, the pose of neutrality dropped. He'd like to slap this guy around some night in a dark alley. Little friendly love taps in the groin and on the ankles with a baton. Just to see if he could take it as much as he liked to dish it out.

"His name was Ranallo. Then he was a lieutenant." They both knew he was now the commander of Homicide.

"Terrific," said Terry Flynn.

Queeney stared wearily at the beefy detective. "I don't want to make your job harder than it is. I loved Francis. You spend all your life with someone, good times and bad, and you end up loving them because there's nothing else you can do. You can't end up hating yourself."

Flynn stared at the silver-haired man at the desk in front of him. "What about the Brothers?"

"What about them?"

"You guys wrote a lot of shit in the paper today about the death threats, about how the Brothers are conducting a terrorist war against the press. You think it's true?"

"Do you?" said Queeney.

"I don't know anything," said Terry Flynn. "I'm just a cop, lifting one foot ahead of the other."

"Well, it seems reasonable, doesn't it?"

"Murder isn't reasonable," said Terry Flynn.

Peter Markk smiled at that. "It sounds like the tag line of a bad movie."

"That's what it's all about," Terry Flynn said. "Bad movies, bad scenes."

"Illusion," agreed Michael Queeney, who seemed to be speaking to himself.

___9___

A Matter of Communication

At the same moment Desmond Clayton spoke of the threat against his life, Karen Kovac sat in a wing chair in a fussy old apartment on the Southwest Side, listening to Sweeney's widow speak between bouts of tears.

In the kitchen, a neighbor named Emily Ryan was making another pot of coffee. Maureen Sweeney looked as though she could have used a drink. Her eyes were rimmed in red, her nose was red, tears had scarred her cheeks. Her gray hair was matted with neglect and sweat. She was not a large woman and grief had diminished her.

"I had a cold. Before this happened, I—"

She blew her nose again. Tears welled. She wiped them away. She blew her nose again.

Karen Kovac waited calmly. It was the worst part of the business, worse than identification of bodies at the morgue. Here the grief she brought was not sudden, not suddenly over with. Here it lingered, the questions twisting the knife again and again until pain was the only constant left in the world.

When the woman was ready, she nodded her head to Karen.

Karen spoke softly, in an almost shy voice. "Was he threatened?"

"Threatened? By what?"

"Had anyone threatened him? Because of something he had written?"

"Francis? I wouldn't know. A long time ago, we stopped talking about the paper. I was so sick of that damned paper, sick of that life. He worked there twenty-six years. Twenty-six years in the bars, with me out here. I went out with him for a long time, I tried to keep up, I drank with him and his cronies. All they ever talked about was newspapers, about stories this one beat that one on, about who was the best, about . . . crap. All of it was crap. I saw what it was. I

tried to get Francis to see what it was. God, I think I could have gotten him out of the bars if I could have gotten him out of the newspaper."

Then, with sudden bitterness: "That was his real life. The paper. I was like a dream to him. He'd come home like he was visiting me. I didn't even exist to him after a while."

"So you didn't talk about the newspaper? About the stories he was working on?"

"Francis didn't say ten words to me in the past five years. Except here's the car keys or something like that."

Mrs. Ryan came into the room with a pot of coffee and cups on a tray and a carton of nondairy creamer. She poured two cups. "I'll leave you two alone for now," she said.

She lingered, waiting to be invited to stay. No invitation came. She went back to the kitchen.

"Francis."

"Did he . . . did he indicate he was upset . . . about anything?"

"It's hard to indicate anything when you can barely crawl through the front door. I think he owed someone money. He always owed someone money. I found a note in his

pockets once, some figures . . . a name."
Vague. She waved her hand as though clearing a cloud in front of her. Her eyes were weak in the weak light. "I can't remember. He always kept secrets from me. There was the life downtown, the life at the paper, in the bars . . . and there was this out here. What would you call it? Life? So sometimes, he never made it home. He had a shirt in his locker at the paper, he had shaving equipment. Sometimes he just drank all night. Sometimes. . . ." The tone was soft again. "Sometimes I figured he'd run into a woman in one of those bars and went home with her, though I couldn't imagine that would be very appetizing. Even to a prostitute. Francis was not . . . Oh, damn, it doesn't matter now, does it?" Tears again. "It's not going to get better, is it?"

Karen Kovac stared at the black liquid in the cup before her. "No," she said. She had been this close to grief only once, when her father died. There was no point in lying; it never got better.

Jack Donovan sat at the end of the long bar in Miller's Pub on Adams Street. Outside,

the El squealed along the Wabash Avenue tracks, half filled with numbed riders heading to the West Side. The snow-crusted walks were nearly empty. It was after Christmas and the stores along State and Wabash carried sale posters in the windows. Some of the windows were being decorated for spring and Easter clothing. Easter seemed an eternity away. Winter had settled in like a rude old man with loud stories.

Lieutenant Matt Schmidt, when he drank at all, drank Seagram's 7 on the rocks with seltzer. This was his second drink of the evening, and it was his limit. The chief of Special Squad rarely frequented bars anymore. But he and Jack Donovan had a problem and it was just as well to settle it now.

"I know where you stand, Jack," he said gently, without giving up anything. "You're going to have to be the front man again."

"I'll give you as much time as I can."

"I appreciate it." Just a hint of sarcasm.

Both had appeared at the press conference in the civic center in the afternoon, while Karen Kovac and Terry Flynn did what they were supposed to do. Both had been photographed, quoted, prodded like

105

produce in a market. But what were they going to do next? Would mass arrests follow? Did they have a suspect? Were they pursuing leads?

Yes. Of course. Everything was proceeding as quickly as possible to find the killers. Said Commander Ranallo of the Homicide/Sex division of the police department. Said Bud Halligan, the state's attorney. Finally said Matt Schmidt and Jack Donovan, forced to repeat the silly messages over and over for television reporters and pencil pushers.

"It's a mess," Jack Donovan said, staring at his stein of beer.

"Well, I knew it was going to be."

"No, you don't know everything."

Matt Schmidt waited.

"I want to be honest with you. I don't want to sandbag you."

Matt Schmidt said nothing.

"Remember Marcus Elijah?"

"Yeah," said Matt Schmidt. "In the armed robbery."

"It was a frame. We're letting him go in the morning."

Still, Matt said nothing. The bar was bright, the booths darker. At the far end, a

couple of tired-looking executives in rumpled suits were watching the Bulls game on television.

"Is that necessary?" Matt Schmidt finally said.

"He's been inside for six weeks waiting trial. Alec Murphy was picked to do PD for him. Murphy put us in an interesting position."

"Murphy is a wiener," said Matt Schmidt, reflecting the common police attitude toward one of the more flamboyant "do-gooder" lawyers in the city.

"Whatever he is, he has the attention of a couple of people in the media he can go to when he can't work a separate deal. The problem with Marcus Elijah is that Murphy has a half-dozen unrelated eyewitnesses, including a Catholic priest, who place him in Kentucky the night of the robbery."

"Convenient," said Matt Schmidt.

"His mother died in Louisville. The funeral was the night of the robbery."

"And why didn't this come up before?"

"Because Marcus Elijah was ordered by his leader, Jesus Mohammed, to say nothing, to martyr himself until the moment of the trial, when—"

"Christ," Matt Schmidt said. "So the police will end up looking like morons."

"Not to mention our office," Jack Donovan said. "I've tried to explain this to Lee Horowitz but he doesn't trust Murphy. Murphy is an outsider."

"But you do."

Jack Donovan had felt boxed in all day, first by Lee, then by Mario, and now by Matt Schmidt. He was getting tired of it. He answered sharply: "You think I shouldn't?"

Matt Schmidt ran his index finger around the rim of the glass. The ice was melting, the drink was thinning. Outside, the wind pressed against the panes and peered into the bar like a visitor without the price of admission.

"Murphy can whipsaw you one way," Schmidt said slowly. Everyone knew Murphy had a pipeline of good will to the media.

"And John Hague's paper can do it the other way if they find out that Marcus Elijah has been released. Murphy said he won't tell anyone if we drop charges and release Elijah."

"Is that credible?"

"Yes."

"You trust Murphy?"

"I trust his word. I trust it more than I trust Lee Horowitz. Nobody knows about this except you. And someone in my office."

"You can't keep it a secret."

"I can give you a couple of days."

"Why tell me?"

"Because if it blows up before you're ready, you and Flynn and Karen—hell, even Ranallo—are going to be in trouble you didn't expect. I can't stop the trouble coming, but I want you to expect it."

Matt Schmidt grimaced. "You're trying to save your own skin."

"Yes," said Jack Donovan.

He sighed. There was no way out of the problem. Maybe Jack Donovan had told him everything just to see if there was an exit Donovan had missed.

"Murphy is a pain in the ass," Matt Schmidt grumped.

"Yes. We'd have a more perfect system of justice without people like him. No messy defenses, no surprise witnesses, no dropped charges."

"If Murphy keeps his word not to leak

this to the papers, you can hold up the paperwork—"

"The trouble is the jail. Depending on how soon Warden Muffin finds out he's lost one of his boarders. Muffin wants to do in Halligan. He's your friend, not ours."

Muffin was a black man who identified himself clearly with the police. All lawyers, even the prosecutor's office, were enemies. Muffin believed with all sincerity that anyone dumb enough to be locked in Cook County Jail was guilty of something—if not of the crime specified, then of something equally bad.

Matt Schmidt understood then. He smiled at Jack Donovan. "You keep surprising people, Jack. They think you're such a boy scout and then you manage to slip in the knife without making any sudden moves."

Donovan did not smile in return. Matt Schmidt understood; Donovan felt he had been leading the lieutenant of Homicide through a lengthy courtroom examination.

"I'll have to talk to Muffin. On your behalf. And have him hold it down for as long as he can. What an odd alliance, if only they knew about it—Murphy and Muffin."

"Mr. Right and Mr. Wrong," Jack Donovan agreed.

"It's the papers, Jack. That's what screws everything up. If we could just get the job done without worrying about heat from the press . . ."

"But we can't. So we outrun them," Donovan said. "We've got Judge Longo in our pocket; we're going to do the release early before the reporters at criminal courts have their morning coffees. I think it'll work but nothing is leakproof. Maybe you'll have a couple of days."

"That brings it up to the weekend. I was going to take three days off. Gert wanted to meet me out in Galena on her way back from Iowa. Just take a country drive."

Jack Donovan did not respond except to finish his beer and push the stein across the bar. The tall bartender caught his eye, Jack nodded and circled with his index finger, indicating Matt Schmidt and himself.

Matt Schmidt said, "I was only going to have two. But Gert isn't home. I don't like the house when she's not home."

"I know what you mean."

"I'm sorry," Matt Schmidt said, remembering Rita Donovan.

"Do you want another?"

"Keep you company," Matt Schmidt said, almost uneasily.

They made a silent salute with their new drinks and sipped. Matt Schmidt nearly thought to tell Jack Donovan about the mark on the wall in the alley where Francis X. Sweeney was clubbed to death. But he didn't; in that last moment, he remembered he was a cop, while Jack represented the other camp—not the enemy but not the friend either. They were reluctant allies harnessed to the same heavy wagon, dragging the same load.

Which is why Jack Donovan felt betrayed six hours later.

__10__

Graffiti

The telephone had been ringing for a long time. He had incorporated the sound into his dream. In the dream, Rita was calling him. She was desperately afraid; she needed him. She was down to her last dime and he had to answer the phone—he knew he had to answer it. And yet he could not get to the phone. He dragged himself across the room and the phone was farther and farther away. He knew it was she.

Kathleen, in white pajamas, stood at the door. She called him until he opened his eyes. Jack Donovan was not awake yet, but he could see her.

"You have to answer the phone," she

said again, patiently. She had awakened him before in the night.

He groaned, pushed himself up in bed. The room was cold. It was always cold, air-conditioned in summer, cold in winter. It was as bare as a monk's cell. Since he had taken his daughter Kathleen to live with him three years before, he had never slept with a woman here.

"For you," she said again.

"Who is . . . what time is it?" He blinked, tried to focus.

"Three."

It was always three in the morning. He grinned weakly. "Sorry you woke up."

"I'm used to it." Tall and all angles like her mother; nothing of him except the small grin that made everything possible, even the impossible things.

"I guess you are."

The telephone was in the kitchen. A single light cast shadows and gremlins over stove, refrigerator, sink. He took the receiver of the yellow wall phone and pressed it against his ear. "Donovan."

"This is Michael Queeney."

Jack Donovan blinked. The name did not register. He waited.

"Michael Queeney," the voice repeated. "I'm managing editor of—"

"Yes," Jack Donovan broke in. He remembered the name from the obituary of Francis X. Sweeney.

"I want to know—Mr. Hague wants to know—why the police altered evidence."

Jack Donovan waited. It was a policeman's trick. People always wanted to explain themselves. It usually worked. Silence implied that the speaker had not finished. People detested silence; they rushed to fill conversational voids. But in this case, silence was met with silence. Perhaps Michael Queeney knew the rules of the game as well.

"I don't really know what you're talking about," Jack Donovan said finally.

"You were appointed to head up the joint team investigating the murder of our reporter, Francis Sweeney."

"Yes."

"We called Halligan, Halligan gave us your number, he said you'd know about it."

"Know about what?"

"In the alley where Sweeney was killed, there was graffiti, a symbol of the Brothers of Mecca. It had been sprayed out. We got

115

a tip, from inside the department. The police investigating the murder altered the evidence."

"The police sprayed over the graffiti?"

"And that's the same investigative team from Homicide that you're in charge of now. Now what do you have to say about it?"

Jack Donovan stared at the kitchen table, at a bowl of apples in the center of the table. Kathleen's idea. She lectured him about fiber and roughage. She was becoming a nag, the way teenagers are when they are reaching for adulthood and a sense of responsibility.

Jack Donovan said, "I'll have to find out about this. I didn't know a thing about it until you called."

Silence.

"Do you want me to call you back?"

"We have a deadline, Mr. Donovan. We're going to press with this story with or without a statement."

"Are you sure of your source?"

"That's our problem," Queeney said with an edge to his voice.

"Not necessarily," Jack Donovan said. "It would be inflammatory to repeat what you just told me in any case. But what if it

116

turned out not to be true?"

"But it is true," Queeney said. "Like the biblical Thomas, I have placed my own hands upon the wall. I have seen the spray. And there is graffiti beneath it, difficult to make out, but combined with our source's assurance."

"Who is your source?"

"A policeman. Who will remain anonymous for obvious reasons." Donovan knew it was probably true then. Cops had loyalty to partners but rarely to the department unless the department was under attack from outsiders. Cops cheated on each other, lied to each other, played the newspapers against each other for private reasons. It was very reasonable to think that someone in the department had dropped a load on Matt Schmidt for some reason that might have had nothing to do with this case.

Donovan felt the sick churning again in his gut. "When is the latest I can get back to you?"

"Twenty minutes," Queeney said.

"Give me your direct number," Jack Donovan said. He opened the kitchen drawer and found a pencil and scratched the number on the wall next to the telephone.

Queeney hung up first without another word.

Donovan stumbled back into his bedroom and found the notebook and took it back to the kitchen. Kathleen was asleep in her own room. The ability of teenage girls to sleep the clock around amazed Jack Donovan.

He dialed, waited. Schmidt answered the phone in a clear voice, as though he had not been asleep.

Jack Donovan told him about the telephone call. There was a long silence. Too long.

"I suppose I should tell you it didn't happen," Matt Schmidt said.

"Jesus Christ, Matt. I told you my dirty little secret about releasing Marcus Elijah."

"I'm sorry it came up right now," Matt Schmidt said ruefully. "Nothing stays secret long but I didn't want the press guiding the investigation. If the graffiti had been left there, we'd have to arrest the whole Brotherhood of Mecca. This isn't the way to clear a murder investigation."

"Jesus Christ, Matt," is all that Jack Donovan could think to say.

"Some evidence technician must have made the call to the paper," Matt Schmidt

118

said thoughtfully. "I wonder why. Well, it doesn't matter. I'll just deny it."

"I wonder why you did it."

"That's obvious, isn't it?"

"I don't think so."

"We photographed the symbol, took paint scrapings. We have all that. But I didn't want to leave it there. Not after we left the scene and it was crawling with newspapermen. TV. Think what TV would make of it."

"I'm thinking," Jack Donovan said.

"Evidence? Who says it's evidence? It was too neat. It was inflammatory. I want to investigate murders, I don't want to handle race riots. Or witch hunts."

"Now we have a public relations problem," Jack Donovan said dryly.

"No, we don't," Matt Schmidt said. He emphasized the word "we."

"What do you think I should do?"

"I think you should do what you think you should do," Matt Schmidt said. His tone was still even. Matt Schmidt was a calm man by nature, thoughtful, quiet. But now there was an edge to his voice that came with the territory of being a policeman. Jack Donovan had been a cop once.

He understood the tone; he had used it himself talking to assistant state's attorneys.

"I should say that I deny that police altered evidence," Jack Donovan tried.

"That's got a ring to it," Schmidt said.

"Perhaps it wasn't evidence at all. As you said."

__11_____

The Course of Murder

Snow began at dawn.

The storm pushed south, through the northwestern suburbs, extending from Madison, Wisconsin, 150 miles northwest to Des Plaines and Arlington Heights. It was going to snow all day. The flakes blew down small and hard; the wind ripped fiercely down the frozen grid of streets, dancing as though lost in the canyons of the Loop and the near North Side. Everyone was late for work. On the west side, a switch froze open on the Lake Street El, disrupting service for thirty-five minutes while CTA crews thawed the switch with torches, exotic cavemen in the urban wilderness still linked to primitive fire

to make their machines run. A tractor-trailer truck jackknifed on a slick patch of the Kennedy Expressway, which arches south and east from O'Hare Airport. Two people in a Volkswagen were killed when twenty tons of frozen butter encased in the trailer flipped on their car and crushed them. The truck driver was not hurt. The Kennedy Expressway was totally blocked for ninety minutes. The commuter trains were running late, and a power line in Canaryville snapped under its weight of ice, blacking out eight hundred homes for two hours. Lemminglike, the frozen commuters—1.3 million in all—struggled on toward the Loop until finally all the mess was cleared, the offices had their complements of workers, and the snowstorm began to blanket the strangled city in whiteness and silence.

Sergeant Terry Flynn did not make it to the meeting until 9:00 A.M. It was just as well. Karen Kovac was even later.

They had all had time to read the morning papers. Including the story about a police cover-up of the "fact" that the Brothers of Mecca were involved in the murder of Francis X. Sweeney.

The only good thing about the morning

was that Commander Leonard Ranallo of Homicide/Sex was snowbound in St. Louis, where he had gone the night before to deliver a morning talk on new methods of scientific investigation practiced in the Chicago police department.

"Such as using spray paint to cover up graffiti," Terry Flynn said with a cheerful smile. He actually seemed to enjoy the chaos and gloom around him. "I'll bet Sid misses this. You think I should send him a clipping?"

"The case or the snowstorm?" Jack Donovan asked.

"Both. A great fucked-up case and a great fucked-up snowstorm. When people get away from Chicago, they begin to miss it. It's like being a kid. Nobody who actually is a kid likes being a kid. Everyone pushes you around, you can't drive, you can't get drunk without someone getting on your case. But as soon as you're not a kid anymore, you remember what fun it was to be a kid."

"I didn't realize you had become a philosopher," Matt Schmidt said.

"Sure. St. Thomas Aquinas, all those guys. The five proofs of the existence of

God. How many angels can dance on the head of a pin. Go ahead and ask me something."

"Who killed Francis Sweeney?"

"I'll tell you who didn't," Terry Flynn said in the same cheerful voice.

"Well, that's one approach, just pick out everyone who didn't and we find out who did," Schmidt said. He was really annoyed, with Flynn and with himself. He had acted instinctively when Karen Kovac found the graffiti in the alley; would he have done it again? He missed Gert and he wanted to get away from this case. It was too hot and all of them knew it was going to get worse.

"Clayton didn't. I kind of liked him, he's got some guts and some smarts but he is scared shitless by this Jesus Mohammed guy. I think we ought to talk to *him* for starters, guy goes around threatening reporters ought to be ashamed of himself."

Slowly, Terry Flynn filled them in on the threat against a reporter named Desmond Clayton. And then Karen Kovac, wet and cold, came into the squad room, removed her coat, and excused herself. After a couple of minutes, she reentered the room. She looked as though it were springtime outside.

Terry and Karen made their separate reports and Matt Schmidt told Terry Flynn about the graffiti incident. Terry Flynn grinned again. "See? You go around in the world doing good, trying to avoid race riots, and what does it get you but a kick in the ass? Never do good, Matt, just stick to being a cop."

Matt Schmidt stared at Terry Flynn with a steely expression in his eyes until the grin faded. Jack Donovan stood by the window and stared out at the gloomy white snow, at the city towers half-hidden in the billions of flakes swirling down from dark gray clouds. He hated winter; he had lived through too many of them.

For a while, none of them thought of anything to say. They watched the storm piling snow on the city.

"The guy who said no two snowflakes are alike. Do you believe that?" Terry Flynn asked.

Karen Kovac stared at him but didn't answer.

"I think it's bullshit," Terry Flynn continued. "It's like fingerprints. I don't believe every fingerprint is different. I bet there's someone in Fiji right now has got

my fingerprints, my face, my eyes, everything. You ever think about that?"

"No," Karen Kovac said.

Again, silence for a while. "Well," Terry Flynn said. "I think I'm going to go out for a while."

"Where?" asked Matt Schmidt.

"It's too cold to dance. I'm going to talk to Brother Clayton again. I sort of worried him down a little bit. Maybe he's got some more shit to tell me. I don't know. I'll play it by ear."

Matt Schmidt stared at him. "Play what by ear?"

"Looking for clues, Matt, for Christ's sake. Looking for suspects. Lurking with intent to gawk. High mopery. You know, just see what's shaking."

"Should I tell you this is a sensitive case?"

Terry Flynn grinned. It was a schoolboy's grin. "Naw. Don't inhibit me."

He buttoned his jacket and walked out of the office, down the hall to the elevator banks.

For more long minutes after he left the room, they were silent again.

"What do you think we ought to do?" Karen Kovac finally asked.

"Talk to everyone at the paper. Terry has the right idea," Matt Schmidt said. "We've got to direct this investigation, take it away from John Hague's paper, and refocus it. They're pointing it one way and we're pointing it another. Back to the paper. Sweeney traveled in a large circle, he knew a lot of people."

"But it was still a circle," Karen Kovac said.

"Yes."

"His wife thought he owed money to someone."

"Juice," Jack Donovan said.

"Possibly," she said. "It might be gambling too. He went to the track."

"He sounds like the kind of guy my mother warned me not to hang around with," Jack Donovan said.

"I can start going through his things, talk to the editors, start on with his fellow—"

"Yes," Matt Schmidt said, suddenly frowning. Terry Flynn had been too happy leaving the office. Well, he thought, he had known what Flynn was like when he picked him for the Special Squad in the first place. Terry Flynn was the man of action, the loose cannon that sometimes punches a hole

in the right place, even if it was for the wrong reason.

He stood up and got his coat.

Jack Donovan stood up as well. "This doesn't seem to be going anywhere," he said.

"Maybe it's the lull before the storm," Matt Schmidt said.

And he didn't realize how right he was.

12

A New Headline

He was very thin. The record showed
he had served three years for armed robbery and another four years for sale and
possession of dangerous drugs, i.e., heroin.
He was currently party to a suit to re-
cover $65,000 in unpaid real estate taxes
on nineteen pieces of slum property in
the Woodlawn and Kenwood neighborhoods
of the South Side. He claimed that since
the Brothers of Mecca owned the apartment buildings and the Brothers of Mecca was a religious organization, he did
not owe property taxes. His name on the
record sheet was Brason Jason Connolly
Jr. For four years, he had been known as

Jesus X. Mohammed.

He sat at the wooden table in the windowless interview room on the second floor of Area One headquarters off the Dan Ryan Expressway at Fifty-First and Wentworth on the South Side. He wore a dashiki and a very large cowboy hat. His arm had tracks of needle marks. His eyes glittered. His face was calm and he was smiling at the large, bulky, red-faced form of Terry Flynn across the table from him.

It wasn't supposed to happen. That is what Matt Schmidt had said in a very quiet, very cold voice to Terry Flynn a moment before.

Terry Flynn had smiled at the reprimand. "I talked to Clayton again, this guy we got in the interview room had threatened him on one other occasion—"

"Big deal," Matt Schmidt said. "Threats are not acts of violence."

"Fuck it, Matt. Why are we pussyfooting around this thing? This fucking cowboy is one of the bad guys, the kind we put in jail. He sells dope to little kids, he's an extortionist and a race-baiting jiveass three-legged alligator that bites everything that comes across his path."

"I'm in charge, sergeant," Matt Schmidt said.

"Fine. Then be in charge," Terry Flynn said. For a long moment, the two men had been suspended in silence and heavy breathing and the echoes of hard words.

"What if we have to let him go?" Matt Schmidt said.

"You mean the papers," Terry said. "I didn't think about that."

"No. But I have to. We got him now and we can't let him go."

"Good. Every day this asshole is off the streets is one day closer to God and glory," Flynn said.

The arrest had been unexpected. By Matt Schmidt. By Jack Donovan already hurrying across town down snow-clotted streets to Area One from the West Side criminal courts complex.

Most of all, Jesus Mohammed had not expected it. Nor had any of the half-dozen followers of the Brothers of Mecca in the headquarters of Shrine Number 1 on South Drexel Boulevard in the Kenwood neighborhood. If they had, there might have been more trouble than there was.

Flynn and two detectives from Area

One—Kelly and Hauptmann, who had worked with Flynn on the priest's murder the previous year—had walked into the building with subpoena blanks in hand, looking for all the world like process servers.

The first guard, on the front door of the six-room apartment on the top floor of a two-flat that was the "shrine," had barred entry momentarily. Kelly had decked him quietly and removed his pistol and M14 automatic rifle. "Nasty things," Kelly had opined.

They broke the door down. This was not legal entry. The door was steel but the jambs were rotted wood. The door fell in on the living room, nearly hitting Jesus X. Mohammed, who was stoned on a layer of cushions and pillows on the floor. Nearby slept two young women, unclothed, as well as two other men. The place reeked of incense and marijuana smoke. A bottle of Russian vodka, nearly empty, was on the floor next to Mohammed. On one wall was a huge mural showing the symbol of the triangle and the eyes that marked the Brothers of Mecca.

Jesus Mohammed was shoved into the

unmarked car before he was fully awake.

And now he sat, hands shaking, in the windowless room on the second floor of Area One detective headquarters. Flynn had acted, Matt Schmidt thought as they entered the room. Perhaps he had wanted action, something outrageous, to break the case, to break the grip of John Hague and the baying of the press at his heels. John Hague's newspaper bayed scandal involving the death of their reporter and the Brothers of Mecca in 128-point Gothic, and the other newspapers in the city were forced, somewhat reluctantly, to pick up the chase.

Radio and television talk shows in the city carried involved conversation with distinguished journalism professors, sociologists, criminologists, and—oddly—sexual therapists, about the threat to a free press currently lurking in the dark city streets. The intimidation was felt most by the police. The switchboard was flooded with hundreds of calls per hour with suggestions on how the police could combat the black menace.

Matt Schmidt stood at the closed door. Karen Kovac was not present. She was in the morgue of John Hague's newspaper, go-

ing through the byline clippings file of the late Francis X. Sweeney. "Woman's work," she had complained to Matt Schmidt. It was probably true and it had bothered Matt at the time. "We're shorthanded until we get a replacement for Sid," he had explained. "It isn't woman's work; it's Sid Margolies's work but he isn't here."

The interview—as the police called the interrogation in soft euphemism—had begun ten minutes before, after Jesus X. Mohammed aka Brason Connolly had been pulled through a crowd of reporters already camped in the central squad area on the second floor. Someone inside the department had again leaked to the media the fact that Jesus X. Mohammed had been arrested twenty minutes earlier. Hague's paper and the *Tribune* city desk had known about the arrest four minutes before Matt Schmidt did, which did not improve his disposition. Around the central desk area were arrayed the closed-door glass-walled offices of Robbery, Homicide, Auto Theft, General Assignment, Youth, and the other detective squads of Area One.

"Hello, Brason, remember me?" Terry Flynn said cheerfully, reentering the room.

"Man, you can't do what you did," Mohammed said.

"I can do anything, Brason. I'm the poh-leese. We is invincible."

"Shit, my lawyer gonna—"

"Fuck your lawyer, asshole. Now I want to talk to you."

"I don't wanna talk to you."

"You threatened Desmond Clayton."

"I deny that."

"He says so."

"I deny it."

"Well, you deny away," Terry Flynn said, "but I'll take the word of a reporter over a junkie on most Sundays. What are you smoking these days, Brason?"

"My name is Jesus."

"Yeah. And my name is John the Baptist, you blasphemous son of a bitch. You got a lot of tracks on your arm, Brason. Didn't your mama ever tell you that doping is hazardous to your health?"

Mohammed smiled, a sly and catlike smile, one reserved for private amusement.

Terry Flynn felt good. He felt good about the arrest, about cuffing Mohammed, about the ride back to Area One, about leading him through the reporters, about frisking

135

him, now about interviewing him. It was action, it was direct, it meant something. The reporters were all locked out on the other side of the door. There was no heat on them in this room: It was just Jesus X. Mohammed and the cops going at each other.

"You threatened Francis Sweeney," Matt Schmidt tried.

"I ain't threatened nobody," Mohammed said. "Francis Sweeney is a jive honkie, don't know nothing about me, about the Brothers. He deserved to die."

"That's a little violent for someone who doesn't know Sweeney."

"Sweeney is dead. Allah struck him down for profaning the religion of the people. And Allah will strike you down."

"Allah use a baseball bat?" Terry Flynn smiled. "Shit, I thought Allah used lightning."

"Turkey," Mohammed said, slipping gently into a different street argot.

"Sticks and stones," Terry Flynn said. "Why don't you tell us all about how you hate the media, how you're gonna get 'em?"

"I am beyond hatred," Mohammed said.

"I am the incarnation of the Prophet on earth, come to His people."

"The Prophet was a sand nigger, not a real one like you, Brason," Terry Flynn said softly.

Matt Schmidt chewed on his toothpick. Terry Flynn always pushed it, always made it rough. Sometimes it was useful. Matt Schmidt felt upset, out of control. It had begun with spraying out the graffiti of the Brothers of Mecca on the brick wall in the alley. It was not a characteristic thing for Matt Schmidt to do. Everything that had happened since had been skewered, out of synch.

"I want to see my attorney."

"You aren't gonna see anyone, asshole, until I tell—goddamnit, sit down there or I'll cuff you."

"I'm getting out of here."

Flynn pushed with both hands. Mohammed hit the wooden seat hard. He stared at the beefy policeman. "You can't hurt my body. I am out of my body."

"You are out of your mind."

Matt Schmidt broke in: "We want to know about why you threatened Desmond Clayton. We want to know about Sweeney.

137

You got a hit out for Sweeney, right?"

"Allah is the avenger, not I," said Mohammed.

"You threatened Clayton."

"I said he would be punished. He will be punished too. Not by my hand but by the hand of the Prophet, by the hand of He Who is All Things."

"You're the Prophet," said Terry Flynn. "You said it."

"I am who am," said Mohammed.

Terry Flynn said nothing for a moment. "We're going to have a little show in a little while and if Clayton signs on, we're going to put you in the shithouse, shithead."

"What you gonna charge me with?"

"How's murder sound?"

"Sound like you shooting up the same stuff I'm using."

"I use clean needles. How about possession of cocaine?"

"You didn't find no cocaine."

"Sure I did," Terry Flynn grinned.

"You will pay to Allah."

"Matt, I'm going to knock the silly putty out of this silly shit." Terry Flynn got up. Matt Schmidt stood up, held up his hand. "Siddown. Siddown, sergeant."

138

"Fuck this shit," said Flynn. He rushed at Mohammed and Schmidt played his part in the ballet by moving between the prisoner and the policeman. He pushed a red-faced Flynn back. "I said siddown, I mean siddown," Matt Schmidt said, raising his voice. He wondered if someone as streetwise as Jesus Mohammed still could fall for these tricks.

"That white man is crazy," Mohammed said.

" 'Cause you make me crazy, Brason."

"I am Jesus."

"Stop that blasphemous shit, you dirty son of a bitch or I'll break your fucking face open."

"When I lead my people away from here and a thousand years of destruction shall descend upon you and upon the earth while we live in paradise, then you shall see the glory and power that is in me," Jesus X. Mohammed said in a quiet, even conversational tone. The abrupt shift in voice was so sudden that both detectives were thrown by it.

"You're crazy," Terry Flynn said.

"I am divinely insane," Mohammed agreed.

"Which is why when you killed Sweeney, it didn't count against you," Flynn said.

"I didn't kill the honkie motherfucker," Mohammed continued in a sweet voice.

"Why did you let Marcus Elijah hang in jail?"

"Because Marcus is a follower of the true God which is Allah in me," Mohammed said, as though explaining how to use the phone book. "Because we do not recognize the laws of the white men who will not let my people go."

"He didn't do it?"

"None of us is accountable."

"Is that right?"

"I am who am," Jesus X. Mohammed said again.

"Oh, shit, Matt, I can't take this shit, I'm gonna knock his fucking teeth down his throat."

"Siddown, Terry," Matt said absently.

The door to the interview room opened. It was Kelly. "Your man is in the next room," Kelly said to Flynn.

Flynn and Schmidt went to the door. They turned to Jesus X. Mohammed. "Stay there."

"Hey, gimme a smoke."

Flynn threw the pack of Luckies at the table.

"You got a match?"

"Want me to smoke it for you too?"

"I'm hungry," Mohammed said.

"We got bologna sandwiches. That still against your religion? I mean, you don't eat meat, do you?"

"A man's gotta eat," Jesus said, smiling.

"But not gods," Flynn said and closed the door. They walked into the next room. Jack Donovan was waiting. He frowned at Flynn. "Well?"

Terry Flynn said, "He's strung out. His brain is fried jelly."

"Is that all?" said Donovan. "What possessed you guys to do an arrest like this?"

"It seemed like a good idea at the time," said Terry Flynn, enjoying the argument.

"Terry decided to take matters in his own hands."

"Look," Terry Flynn said. "You guys are reasonable, cautious, all that—and all it's getting us is Ranallo on our case and the papers and all this shit because Hague's people want to hang the Mecca Brothers. Fine. Let them hang 'em."

"It doesn't work that way," Jack Donovan

began, his feet planted in the middle of the floor of the squad room. "The way it works is that we try to find the guilty guy first."

"Listen, Brason is guilty of something," Flynn said.

"You're not listening, Terry. We charge him with anything in connection with Sweeney's murder, we have to come up with evidence. We don't have any evidence. And we let him go, the papers are worse than they were before."

"So what do you want to do?"

"Jesus, Terry."

"No. Me no Jesus. Jesus in the interview room."

Jack Donovan's jaw worked back and forth a moment. "You're a fucking asshole sometimes, Terry," he said at last.

Flynn flushed but did not move.

Matt Schmidt had not taken part in it because he was still waiting. For something.

"What do you want to add to this mess, Matt?" Jack Donovan said at last.

"I don't know. If we go through the process, can we hold him?"

"No," Jack Donovan said. "Not unless you know something more than I've heard so far."

"Well, can we just—"

"No," Jack Donovan said in a flat voice. "Terry Flynn gets you into a mess and now I'm supposed to get you out of it, but it doesn't work that way. Why the hell do you suppose the Man on Five wanted to put together this bullshit special team in the first place? To redirect the heat away from him. And Halligan does not want it on him. The cops are holding the bag of shit at the moment."

"We get used to it," Terry Flynn said. "From all the super prosecutors we got in the SAO."

"Terry, this was dumb," Jack Donovan said coldly. "You got bored, you picked up one of the most inflammatory black leaders in the city. On what? A verbal threat allegedly made by him against a reporter?"

Terry Flynn understood but he wasn't going to back down. "Brason is a scumbag. He should be killed on general principles of humanity. He's a dope pusher, a mother-fucker, and father-raper. Scum. Take a guy like Clayton, he's going to be pushed around by someone like this turd? Clayton is a black guy and that makes him different, right? You got a white reporter beaten to death

and we got to be careful of everyone's civil rights, especially when it's the rights of the black Adolph Hitler in there. But what about Clayton? He was threatened twice. With death. By this scumbag who's already spent time in the joint for unspeakable acts. You see how it works, Jack? You're worried about Bud Halligan and Matt, you're worried about Ranallo. Me, I'm not worried. You wanna put me on a beat in Kensington guarding the cemetery, fine, fuck both you and everyone who looks like you. You know Clayton's father was a delegate to the UN? He was a scientist? This guy put it on the line. I don't like reporters, I still don't, but gimme fifty Claytons over shit like we got sitting in the interview room, stinking it up."

Matt Schmidt was surprised, not for the first time. So, this was all about Clayton. It had worried at Terry Flynn until he had acted—not on behalf of Sweeney, but to scare off Mohammed from Clayton.

"I don't believe you," Matt Schmidt said slowly. But he was smiling, slightly, in a sour way.

"Sure, I'm full of surprises," Terry Flynn said. "Well, Jack, are you gonna take it

back about me being an asshole?"

"No," Jack Donovan said. "This was not a good idea."

The three men waited.

"If it wasn't this one or one of his men, who was it?" Jack Donovan said.

"A random act, like we thought before. Or someone he knew. Involved in the paper. Someone he owed money to."

Jack Donovan said, "I can take care of it."

Matt Schmidt looked surprised. "I didn't expect a volunteer from the state's attorney's office."

Jack Donovan shrugged. In a little while, he would be cornered by Lee Horowitz, screaming about the police double-crossing the state's attorney's office, about altering evidence, about not caring enough about resolving the problem of Sweeney's death. Donovan thought of Sweeney, of the photographs of the fat man's body arched in death on the bricks of a snow-covered alley. His death was a problem, that's all. His widow wept for him and the newspaper wept for him in print, but he was mostly a problem.

"I can't hold him," Jack Donovan said.

145

"But maybe I can deflect it a little. Is Clayton here?"

"He's coming."

"I'll call up Burt at the U.S. attorney's office," Jack said. "He owes me one."

Matt Schmidt nodded. "Yes. That would work."

"Burt can take it, he's immune. He can announce an investigation based on evidence we're supplying. The possibility of civil-rights violations. Something like that. It's all crap but it should read all right. Bud gets off the hook for today. Even you guys get off the hook. But Terry, don't do that again."

"It's hard to promise," Terry Flynn said. "I'm so unpredictable."

____13_____

The Killing

Alec Murphy, public defender, reached into his pocket for a twenty and handed it to the sullen-faced young man next to him in the car.

Marcus Elijah accepted the note with dull eyes and no thanks. He stared out the window at the winter-gray street corner, piled with snow. More snow was still falling. It was just after eleven.

"This is where you wanted to be dropped," Murphy said. He had owlish glasses and a rock jaw and dancing green eyes. An hour earlier, after the court hearing, Marcus Elijah had been released from County Jail at Twenty-sixth and California.

Now Murphy's battered gray Ford was parked in a no-parking zone on the corner of Garfield Boulevard and Stewart on the South Side.

"Yeah. This is where I want to be dropped. I got me a sister live up there," Marcus said. "I still don't see why they let me go."

"Because you didn't do it. Because they made a mistake," Alec Murphy said in an even voice. He was getting a little tired of Marcus Elijah.

"I didn't do it before," he said. "But that didn't stop me spendin' six weeks in the place."

"Look, Marcus. You knew you were in Kentucky when the robbery went down, how come you never offered an alibi? This is all bullshit. The SAO did the right thing and you got out of jail despite yourself. I know you had some caca idea about dumping on the cops if you went to trial. So don't give me shit, okay?"

"Hey, fuck you too, motherfucker."

Alec Murphy shook his head. You got used to it. Even the abuse. It all just saddened him, confirming year by year his deep and abiding hatred of his fellow man, even

as he struggled in the law on behalf of the poor and left-out. Sometimes he thought he was really doing it for himself, for some inner need as persistent as an itch, and not for scum like Marcus Elijah. When he thought those things, he felt sorry for himself. He felt sorry for himself now.

"Go on, Marcus, go on. I hope I don't see your ugly face anytime soon."

"You some jive—"

"Try me," Alec Murphy said. "I get real tired of you real easy."

Marcus Elijah opened the car and felt the hawk biting in the wind. He buried his bare hands in the pockets of his light jacket and headed across the street against the light, slipping on the new-fallen snow. Snow chips battered his face, blinded him a moment. He took several steps, turned; the gray Ford was already around the corner, treading slowly through the cautious traffic, heading west back to the Criminal Courts Building and the County Jail.

Chump, thought Marcus Elijah. Jiveass honkie chump. He'd seen that face before, those glasses, chump's face.

Looking for Billie now, she'd been living up the block six weeks ago. An hour with

Billie, then time to see ole J.C., the living Prophet himself, find out what's going down. J.C. owed some money, he'd taken that fall on the robbery, the living Prophet had some dimes to come across. Big dimes. Take the money and get outta this mother-fucking city for the winter, go on down toward home. But first there was Billie.

All the mailboxes in the sagging frame four-flat were ripped from the wall. Holes in the wall served as temporary mailboxes but no one wrote to anyone inside. Except the gas company wanting to shut off the gas or the electric company wanting to shut off the electric. Even the old people who lived in two rooms in the back had the social-security check sent to the bank now.

The wooden stairwell smelled of urine and mice.

On the second landing, a door painted a hideous orange hid the front apartment. He banged on the door and waited a long time.

"Whozat?"

"Billie? That you?"

"Whozat?"

"Say, baby. Me. Marcus."

"Marcus who?"

"Shit, baby. You ain't forgot me. I was gone. You know. In the place. Come on, baby. Open up."

"Marcus? Marcus?"

"That's right."

"Marcus. Can't open up right now. I can't do it right now."

"Can't do it right now? What's you saying, baby? Come on, baby, I gotta get inside." Smiled. "Come on, baby, it's me."

"Marcus? I can't open up right now. How come you come now?"

The smile faded, slowly. A frown grew. "Billie. You trickin' in there? You got some chump in there?"

A deeper voice. "Who you? Who you callin' a chump?"

Marcus Elijah took a step back. Considered the door. "Who want to know?"

"I ain't no motherfuckin' chump, chump." The door opened.

He was large, shirtless, hairy. He had wild eyes.

Billie was not naked. She wore a sweater. Her eyes were glittering. Marcus saw she was flying, she was really on the other side of the moon now. Marcus saw she didn't know if she was fucking or sucking or just

rolling in snow. The cow jumped over the moon and the little dog laughed to see such sport. . . .

"Man, you ain't wanted 'round here, just go on 'bout your business."

"Who you?" Resentment, even curiosity. Not anger. Marcus Elijah was not angry.

"Ain't nothin' for you to know 'cept that you interferin' with me."

"Say, man, I got a claim on that girl—"

Billie giggled, put her hand to her mouth. The big man half-turned. "Shut your fuckin' mouth, bitch."

Giggled.

Marcus took a step, thought about it. He was big. But Marcus was just curious.

"What you want?"

"I want? Say, I don't care. You know. Your business. I been in the place two months, I need some shit, you know? You got anything to share?"

"What d'I look like? Salvation Army, nigger?"

"Shit, man. It's cold, the man just dropped me out here, I was looking to get warm, shit, I ain't even got a dime, I sure could use—"

"Man, get the fuck away from my face,

you unnerstand?"

"Aw, man."

The big man pushed, slightly. It was absurd. Marcus Elijah was twenty-three. He had killed a man when he was eleven, his first killing. He had survived it all, survived the fights, the initiations, the ghetto streets that stretched back all his life. Absurd. He merely slipped.

Fell back.

Struck his head on the wooden balustrade at the top of the stairs, which dizzied him but did not knock him out.

The problem was one of balance.

He hadn't braced for the slight push because he wasn't threatening the big man at the door, he was curious, he saw Billie's eyes glittering, he knew some shit was sending her over the moon, he wanted a little, you know . . .

Stupid. He was falling backward because there was no support. He reached for the rotten handrail and it came loose and then it couldn't be stopped, he would just have to sail along down the stairs, just sail like doing a backstroke to the edge of the pool in Washington Park, just sail like a cloud or balloon. . . .

Halfway down the stairs, he broke his neck.

And there was no reason for it at all.

14

A Reporter's Secrets

Karen Kovac had been married. She had a son who was now visiting her ex-husband for the day. He was an advertising executive, and when he had married Karen Wisniewski, he had done so for a simple reason: He loved her. In his way.

His way turned out not to be hers. It was not easy, especially after her son, Tim, was born. She had broken from her husband, divorced him, kept the child, become a policewoman. Why that? her husband had asked at the divorce hearing. Why a policewoman?

She could not have answered. It was one of a hundred things she had tried to do and

the only thing that had been opened to her. She had three years of college, enough to become a secretary. She didn't want that, she didn't want to do the things she was qualified to do. She never spoke of women's liberation; in fact, she rarely thought about it. All she wanted was to be free herself and this was the easiest way to do it.

She had not intended to become Terry Flynn's lover. He was not her sort. More important, she saw him as a limited man, as limited in a different way as her former husband. He had no great ambitions; her former husband had too many. But Terry Flynn's mere contentment at his lot in life infuriated her as much as her husband's ambitions had. She could not explain it to anyone. She wanted to be herself, alone, to raise her son, to have a life apart from others that would satisfy her in the end. She knew it was selfish of her.

Terry Flynn had been a complication from the beginning. The problem was simple: she wanted him.

He kissed her now.

His large body covered her.

She felt his weight descend on her. She opened her legs to him. They were lovers

without experiments, lovers of few words, lovers as familiar as old married couples. Except those were not the things that interested Karen Kovac. Someday, she thought, she would have to break off the relationship. Someday, she would leave Terry Flynn.

Karen Kovac had realized from the beginning that Terry Flynn would never leave her.

He had been married but he never spoke of it. It had to do with Vietnam, coming home, being changed and restless, becoming a policeman, burying some part of himself uncovered in the war in the tomb of his job. Freezing out his young wife from the war and the job, from the world of men and the world of violent things. It had been too much for his wife to take and too much to expect her to take. He had understood that, even as it saddened him. Terry Flynn was not given to self-doubt except in matters of importance.

"There," said Karen Kovac in her low voice, her back arching up to meet him, her lips buried in the crook of his neck as he covered her. There. She felt the warmth seep into her. It was cold, cold against the

windowpanes and on the bedroom floor. But now, in this moment, there was warmth.

"There," she said.

He did not say he loved her. They understood, both of them, that it wasn't necessary. He did not speak to her when they made love nor, for a long time, after love. He felt awkward with her at times, aware of his bulk, his profanity, his beery breath, his unkempt appearance. She seemed like a diamond to him or a picture of a beautiful woman. She was cool and sure, and her frown was more potent than rage from another person. She was precise, he thought. He felt like an intruder at times.

But not when they made love. Not when she was so strong and her legs held him and her body pushed into his body and they were joined and he could feel her sharp teeth on his neck and her lips kissing him as she bit him. In those moments, it was never awkward between them, as though in their separate, even lonely lives apart, the distinctions only blurred, pleasantly, when they came together.

"If you want a can of beer, have a can of beer," Karen Kovac said, wrapped in a cot-

ton robe, her feet curled under her, on the couch by the bay window of the old courtyard building on the Northwest Side. Across the courtyard, another window, without lights, stared glumly over at them. She had lived in the building for six years and there was a rumor that it would go condo in the spring. She hoped not; she could not afford to buy her apartment.

Terry Flynn patted his bare belly. "No. I had that wine. I'm cutting down. Haven't you noticed?"

"Yes," she said, which was a lie.

"Well, maybe one."

He padded to the kitchen on bare feet and opened the refrigerator. The apartment was still save for the faint sounds of Beethoven on the small stereo in the dining room. He could stay all night because Tim would be at his father's overnight. Tim knew about Terry Flynn, probably knew about their affair; but Karen Kovac maintained a rigid decorum. She had ideas about raising Tim that came from the roots of her Polish-American family.

He wore a large bath towel around his middle.

"Aren't you cold?" she said, snuggling

next to him when he sat down beside her on the couch. He tasted the beer and smiled like a kid. "No. Always was warm-blooded, you know that. Women are the only cold-blooded people."

"We have to be," Karen Kovac said.

"You got that out of Betty Friedan," Terry Flynn responded. He felt at ease with her now, after making love.

"I didn't know you knew about Betty Friedan."

"I even know about Mao Tse-tung but that doesn't make me a Communist."

"No one would ever accuse you of being into women's liberation."

"You're wrong, Karen. All kinds of people accuse me of it. Sid. I just thought about Sid. He's been gone a couple of days and it's like he was gone a year."

"Makes you think that's the way it'd be if you went away."

"I could stand California. Especially after today. We got almost a foot of snow."

"It's like dying," Karen Kovac said.

He turned to look at her. "What's like dying?"

"Going to California."

"Like dying and going to heaven."

But she was in a sort of reverie, not really listening to him. "We saw Sid every day and when he's gone, he's just gone. He might have been gone a year. When my father died, I was sure I'd never forget him. And I do remember him but it gets dimmer all the time."

"Like yesterday's newspaper," Terry Flynn said.

She was surprised and showed it. "You knew what I was thinking of."

"Yeah. I'm a mystic."

"Francis Sweeney. I spent two days with him. I saw his body, I read the coroner's report. I was at his apartment, I talked to his wife, I spent all day at the paper. I talked to Michael Queeney. They started at the paper together. And I even talked to John Hague. And that reporter, Clayton. And there was the stuff in his desk. He might have been dead a year. They all talked about him as though they barely remembered him. Nobody speaks ill of the dead."

"Well, Sid was a pain in the ass sometimes," Terry Flynn said playfully.

She smiled. "I talked to Michael Queeney again. About Sweeney. He said the paper was actually thinking of firing him."

161

"Is that right?"

"Yes. He was so direct. He was very honest. He said he had loved Francis, that Francis had felt alienated from him in recent years. He said that Francis was a drunk—we knew that—he said that he had tried to hold onto Sweeney's job for him. . . ."

"He sounds like a self-described saint."

"No," Karen Kovac said. "I don't think so. He said he saw a lot of himself in Francis. I said, 'How do you mean?' He said something about struggling along, day after day, you never got tired of the daily fix. He said journalism was like taking a drug. You needed the high and if you didn't get it, it flattened everything out for you. He said that he needed it as much as Francis did, even if Francis had come to hate it. I think I understood what he meant."

"Helluva lot of philosophy. What's it got to do with whoever killed Sweeney?"

"I don't know. I was thinking about what you said. That there was somebody who looked just like you in Fiji or someplace on the other side of the world. That all the fingerprints aren't different." She closed her eyes to see her thoughts better. "I was try-

ing to understand Sweeney and he was so far away already. I looked through his desk. Did I tell you that? He had a bookie, I got a lot of numbers. He also owed someone money. There were notations. It took me a while to figure out. Someone named Theodore. I called his wife, she said it might have been the name she saw on a sheet of paper with numbers on it. I was going to mention it after I saw Mrs. Sweeney again."

"Theodore?"

She turned to him. The room was filled with the gentleness of Beethoven's *Pastoral*. All else was silence; even the wind had died.

"Do you know something about someone like that?"

Terry Flynn said, "There's a character named Theodore. He was a boxer. Wears lavender perfume. His name was Mr. Theodore, he was a collector for the Outfit."

"Juice?" she said.

"Yeah."

"My God." She said it softly, as soft as a child wrapping his hand around a sparrow with a broken wing. They had been feeling around the case like blind people in darkness. Now it was suddenly there, something solid, something clearly before them.

"Yeah," said Terry Flynn. "Maybe this is what this is all about. Maybe he had it right there in his notes after all."

___15___

Newspaper Murders

The story on page one was illustrated by a six-column headline in three lines. The headline consisted of 144-point Gothic (heavy) type, of the sort used to announce the commencement of wars or their end. It related the bare fact that a second murder involving the Brothers of Mecca had been revealed.

The final edition of John Hague's newspaper hit the street at four in the morning.

An attempt by the city desk to reach Jack Donovan for comment on the "vicious beating death of cult figure Marcus Elijah" two days after a similar bludgeoning of reporter "Francis X. Sweeney, whose crusading se-

ries on the drug empire of the outlawed Brothers of Mecca" had presumably been "linked by police and special investigators from the state's attorney's office" failed. Jack Donovan had removed the telephone jack from the wall after receiving midnight harangues from Leonard Ranallo (still trapped by the snowstorm in St. Louis) and Lee Horowitz, leaving it unplugged until the next morning. Horowitz had wanted to know why Jack Donovan had dropped charges against Marcus Elijah in the first place.

Jack Donovan had said because Marcus Elijah was innocent.

Lee Horowitz had fumed that Marcus Elijah was a drug-shooting scum whose natural habitat was County Jail and that any decision to drop charges should have been made by the First Assistant (Lee Horowitz) and not by a man allegedly directing a special investigation into the death of a newspaper reporter.

When Ranallo learned—in a phone call from Matt Schmidt—of Marcus Elijah's death, he said much the same thing, only from the police point of view.

"Since when does a pimp shit like Alec

Murphy carry more weight with the SAO than the fucking police?" is the way Leonard Ranallo had phrased it.

Jack Donovan had been smiling when he hung up, and Kathleen asked him what it was all about.

"I don't know. It's so bad right now that it can't be as serious as it seems," Jack Donovan replied. And removed the telephone wire from the jack and went to bed.

Morning was white and the sky clear and full of sun. The breath of the storm had cleaned away the fumes of city life and blown them across Lake Michigan to the Michigan shoreline, which was now being battered by snow. The city seemed calm under the blanket of white. On the arterial streets, giant blue-painted garbage scows fitted with plows shoved the snow out of the way of buses and cabs and long lines of cars and tractor-trailer trucks caught on the maze of streets. A mountain of rock salt on the south bank of the Chicago river near the harbor entrance was steadily being reduced by plow trucks that had been treading back and forth across the city all day and night, spraying salt on the streets like farm ma-

chines spreading seeds on a field in spring. The salt would melt the snow and bleach the streets and eventually help water work its way under the asphalt so that, in spring, constant expansion and contraction of water would tear the streets into potholes that would be patched all summer to prepare for another winter of snow and salt.

Jack Donovan took the Kennedy line El train to the Loop. He got off at the Randolph subway station shared with the Milwaukee Avenue line and marched through the connecting tunnel that led to the Civic Center. The whole of the Loop was a maze of tunnels like this, burrowed from building to building over the years, used during the long twilight of the Chicago winter.

It was time, Jack Donovan had decided, to see Lee Horowitz and explain the situation. In Jack Donovan's terms.

He had read the morning papers on the El.

Including the ludicrous hysterics of John Hague's paper. Ludicrous because Matt Schmidt had telephoned him at seven with a helping of good news.

Lee Horowitz's secretary looked up as

Jack entered; she smiled vaguely and said hello.

Jack Donovan, for a change, did not speak. He pushed through the outer office to Lee Horowitz's inner office. Lee was alone at the immense desk (a desk larger than his boss's down the hall). Lee Horowitz owned the rosewood desk and had had it moved specially into his office when Halligan won the job ten years before. On the wall behind Lee Horowitz were photographs of Lee standing with various politicians, posing and smiling. One of them was the mayor, and it had center position. Slightly off center behind Lee was a photograph of Lee Horowitz shaking hands and slapping the back of Harry S Truman. It was inscribed from Truman. More important, the photograph with the mayor was also inscribed.

"Hello, Lee."

Leland Horowitz looked up from the editorial page of the *Tribune* and frowned.

"What do you want?"

"I want you to back off. Back off me and back off this investigation."

"Why?"

"Marcus Elijah."

"The guy you let go. The guy that gave John Hague a headline this morning. The creep that—"

"Marcus Elijah's killer was picked up three hours ago."

Lee Horowitz gaped. Then the frown resumed control and deepened. He waited without a word and Jack Donovan paced to the window wall and looked out at the plaza below. In the stunning dry cold air, pedestrians scurried across the plaza. On one side of the square was the giant, rusting hulk of the Chicago Picasso statue, which resembled either a dog or a woman, depending on the angle from which it was seen. The other side of the plaza had an eternal flame in memory of John F. Kennedy that was snuffed out from time to time by the vicious winds that circled around the plaza, the high-rise Civic Center, and the block-long City Hall and County Building across the street.

"We've been too easy," Jack Donovan began. "John Hague's paper is pushing us this way and that, which makes any kind of investigation nearly impossible."

"The police destroyed evidence. . . ."

"Bullshit. That's what John Hague said.

I've talked to Matt Schmidt, to the other detectives and uniformed officers at the scene. No one saw any graffiti. For all I know, John Hague's people made it up."

"Jack, I been around forty years, I know every lie in the book. I wrote most of them. You're lying, the cops are lying, but I don't give a fuck, just so you don't think you're fooling me. He got a call from a police informant and you and I know it, so let's let it drop."

"Lee. The paper says it got a call from a cop. Show me the call. Tell me his name."

"This is bullshit, Jack. You're covering up. The cops are lying and you're lying as well."

"No," Jack Donovan lied.

Lee knew it. "Damnit, Jack."

"What do you want to say? Let's be honest with each other? It's late for that, Lee."

"I've backed you, Jack, you know that, when your ass was in a sling."

"With friends like you, Lee . . . ," Jack Donovan said, not finishing the thought. "The point is that John Hague has pushed it too far this time. He linked the death of his reporter with Marcus Elijah's death and printed the rantings and ravings of Jesus

171

Mohammed yesterday to buttress his argument. But the whole thing falls down now that we picked up the man who killed Marcus."

"So tell me."

"He's in the lockup now. Two dicks from the South Side named Hauptmann and Kelly picked him up. It was complicated but it was fairly simple."

"What's his connection with Sweeney?"

"None, Lee. You're talking like one of Hague's reporters. You work for the state, not the newspapers."

"Jack, you don't know a damned thing about this office. You don't. You couldn't run for dogcatcher, you're so fucking dumb sometimes."

Jack Donovan's face turned pale but he waited Lee out.

"Dumb. You think Bud Halligan is anointed state's attorney? You think he inherited his job like a fucking English prince gets to be queen? Bud Halligan did his precinct work, he rang the bells, he gave out the literature, he counted the votes until they came out right. He worked right up the ladder in a lot of dirty jobs, he shook a lot of sweaty hands, he drank dago red with

172

the dagos and beer with the turkeys and ate pirogis with the Polacks. He danced at their weddings and said the rosary at their wakes. Now he's slated but he's a Democrat, which is okay for the city but this is a county office and there are Republicans out there in the country towns. So he's got to keep the shines in one pocket and keep the whitebreads in another and not mix them up. And the papers. He's got to have the papers. A state's attorney fucks the papers and the papers fuck him back and that's that. You know this office at least, you know the way things really work. Well, we need the papers to keep the fiction going. You know, Justice and Truth and blah-blah-blah. So you think John Hague has gone too far? How about if John Hague or the *Trib* or the *Daily News* decided to go after Bud Halligan the way Hague is going after the Brothers of Mecca? Say he says, 'We're going to hang that fucking turkey asshole'? You know what happens? They do it. Just like that. The press is a lynch mob always on the street, looking for someone to hang. The smart thing you got to do is make sure you're part of the mob, not one of the people gonna be hanged. It may not be fair but

fair don't count when you got a rope around your neck. Then it's just dead."

Lee Horowitz had begun the outburst with breathless anger but when he finished, his voice had softened. He was telling the truth for a change and both of them knew it.

Now Jack Donovan spoke quietly: "A woman named Billie Raye called the cops about three because her old man had beaten her up and locked her out of the apartment and she was mad and she was cold. The beat cops noticed it was the same building where Marcus Elijah had been found in the hallway in the afternoon. One thing led to another, and it turns out her old man is named Frank Thurmon; and after a while, Billie Raye lets out that Frank pushed Marcus Elijah down the stairs accidentally on purpose. Then he decided to cover it up by beating up on Marcus's poor old body. Dumb but not so dumb either. Maybe Frank read the papers the way you do."

The last was delivered flatly; the sting was in the words.

Lee took it, his face flushed.

"The point, Lee, is that there are two or three leads on this thing with Sweeney and

the cops need a little breathing room if they're going to do anything about it. That means you going to bat against John Hague and Leonard Ranallo and all the rest of them. And going to the Fifth Floor if you have to. I'm not ambitious, Lee. I didn't want this investigation."

"We were going to be forced into it. You know that. It looks good in the papers, the forces of law and justice united."

"Yes. I know, Lee. I know all about it."

"I got one question, Jack."

Donovan stood at the floor-to-ceiling windows and stared at the pedestrians below and waited.

"Is it going to be all right, Jack?"

"What do you mean?"

"Bud. Bud puts his ass on the line, blocks the interference, is it going to work out all right? I mean, are we going to clear this thing? Are we going to have some satisfaction for the risk?"

"I don't know, Lee. You know that."

"What do the cops think?"

"They don't know."

"Nobody knows, Jack, right? Nobody knows nothing but you know you want to see Bud stand up to the papers and the Man

on Five and the police superintendent and you know that it might mean nothing. Like the guy in Watergate dangling in the wind. He puts it on the line and they walk away from him. Why should Bud do this?"

"Because it's the only way anything is going to get done," Jack Donovan said softly, feeling the gorge rising again, feeling his stomach ache again. He had felt certain when he entered the office to see Horowitz; he had identified Horowitz as the enemy of the moment. But now Lee was mitigating the anger Jack Donovan had counted on to carry him through.

"If Bud—if you, Lee, it's the same thing—don't keep those guys at bay, if they don't let us get on with it, we're never going to find out who killed Francis X. Sweeney. And six months from now, when the heat has died down, the papers are going to be making endorsements for state's attorney and they're going to remember that Bud Halligan's special team let them down. You know it and I know it. So take the heat now or take it later."

"Maybe you aren't so dumb," Lee Horowitz said at last. It was not a commitment but Jack turned then and thought he saw

the trace of a grudging smile at the corners of Lee's mouth.

Maybe, Jack Donovan thought, he was going to get the time after all.

__16_____

Mr. Theodore

He weighed three hundred pounds and was
nearly six foot four. He had gray hair and
eyes that were large and set flatly on either
side of his large nose—a nose that had never
been broken, even after forty-eight fights.
Even after years in his peculiar trade as a
juice collector.

He smelled of lavender. He might have
bathed in it. He wore a flowered shirt,
as though it were summer, open at the
neck. Around his neck was a golden chain
affixed to a large crucifix as well as a St.
Joseph medal. His blue sport coat was cashmere.

He sat at the bar in the Vernon Park

Tap in the Italian area of the old West Side called Taylor Street. The Tap was a neighborhood place with a large, bare dining room in the back where the city's quiet gourmets usually found the best pasta.

It was noon and the bright, cold day continued to flood the city streets with unaccustomed winter cheerfulness.

Mr. Theodore smiled. His teeth were beautiful and large.

"Sure, he had my name down. I knew the bum. I knew him for years. He did a profile about me once. You know."

Sergeant Terry Flynn sat across from him, chewing on a toothpick. Karen Kovac stood near him but she had not spoken.

"Any of it true, Theodore?"

"Well, you know." He smiled again. His voice sounded like an unoiled machine in constant use. "It was a newspaper story, a nice story, you could give it to your mother to read. It was mostly true. I mean, for a newspaper, you know."

"He owed you money."

Theodore blinked, the smile remained. "Hey, I don't think so."

"Sure he did."

"Naw. I don't think so. Besides, he's dead, ain't he? When you're dead, you don't owe nobody nothing. It's like bankruptcy. Yeah. I like that, you like that?"

"How much he owe you?"

"Look, now and then, he'd borrow a nickel. You know, he had a DWI beef last year, he needed a grand to put it down, you know."

Terry Flynn grinned. He had felt relieved from the moment Karen Kovac mentioned his name found in Sweeney's notebook. He could understand someone like Michael Vincent Teatettero aka Mr. Theodore.

"What was the juice?"

"Hey, everybody pay juice, you know. Since the Arabs, fucking stupid Arabs, since they fucked with the gasoline, everything goes crazy. You go to a bank now, you need a loan, you know what it's gonna run you in juice? Listen, borrowing from the street gets cheaper than First National Bank or something."

"Did he pay you back?"

The grin faded, slowly. Theodore reached for the glass of tomato juice and his giant sausage fingers entombed it. He raised the glass to his thick, purple lips and tasted.

"He owed a few dimes. No big thing."

"He paying? I mean, before he checked out?"

"Well, to tell you the truth, sergeant, he was slow."

"Slow enough to get some bridgework done?"

"Naw. He was a newspaper guy. High-risk loan. I did it as a favor. Those guys are fun, you know, I go hang out once in a while, down at Riccardo's, over to Billy Goat, I listen to them. They're like babies but they're funny, some of them. I liked Sweeney. I'm going to the wake tonight. Way da fuck out south, excuse my language, lady."

Karen Kovac did not speak.

"That's an attractive coat," Mr. Theodore said, grinning. "It looks nice on you."

"Theodore, it's too late for charm school. Tell me about Sweeney."

"Okay. I was sort of waiting for someone to come talk to me."

"But you weren't going to step forward out of turn," Terry Flynn said.

"I maybe got hit too hard in a few fights but I ain't gone dizzy yet. I lay it on you the way it is, sergeant." The voice rasped on.

"Sweeney, I liked him. We'd go to the fights. Golden Gloves, anything, even that shit up at Aragon Ballroom, fucking Puerto Ricans they look like babies fighting each other in a nursery school or something. Sweeney is one of the losers, you know? If he didn't know how to write, he'd be a bag lady. But he was sweet. He was a wise guy but he was okay. Sure, I'd drop some bread on him and he always paid it back. I think he liked the idea of owing me money. Made him feel . . . well, I dunno. Whatever turns you on, you know?"

"You get mean to him?"

"Naw. None of that. I remind him sometimes. You know. He'd come through. So I figure you want to know if I wasted him?"

"Yeah."

"That's what I figured."

"Well?"

"No."

"Honest to God? Swear on your Godfather's grave?"

"Yeah I swear. Man, you think I'd kill someone like him? A fucking newspaper guy? I'd be writing my own death notice."

"Stranger things have happened."

"I tole you, I ain't gone punchy. The

only thing I knew about Sweeney was what I read in the papers. Some guys killed him. You know, the *tutsones* with the crazy religion."

"No. We don't think that."

"Fuck, think what you want. Except I'd do him. You talk to your pals in the peeper detail. They know about me, about my friends and . . . associates. We got no beef with Sweeney."

"Talk to me, Theodore, I'm not talking to anyone else but you right now," Terry Flynn said.

"Hey, fuck, man, don't go with that stuff."

"Shut the fuck up, apeman, when I'm talking to you."

"Hey, man, what are you doing, talking like that in front of the lady? Shit, take it easy, will ya? Now, I didn't do Sweeney. Next off, I don't need no fucking baseball bat or whatever. If I wanted to tear Sweeney up, I'd just use my hands, you know that, you know all about me, don't tell me you don't."

"I saw you fight right at the end," Terry Flynn said.

"Yeah?" Uninterested. His large eyes

were bored, lazy. "I wasn't at my best then."

"Not like now, huh?"

"I take care of myself. I got a weight problem. That's all. I work at it. I run, I work out, I drink so much fucking tomato juice I'm turning into a tomato juice. I beg your pardon."

Karen Kovac smiled suddenly and Mr. Theodore replaced his grin.

"That's a very attractive purse," he said.

"A fucking purse?" Terry Flynn said.

"Cops. You never say nothing nice to anyone. It's why cops get divorced all the time."

"He's right," Karen Kovac said. She couldn't help smiling.

Mr. Theodore's grin was broad as a shark's. "I liked Sweeney, I knew him for years, on my mother's grave."

Karen Kovac said, "Who else?"

"Who else what?" Still grinning.

Terry Flynn said nothing.

"Who else did you know for years? Do you know?"

"Lots of people, lady." Softly. The beginning of a wary tone.

"Like who else?" Karen Kovac said.

"I don't understand."

"Hanging around. With the newspaper people. Riccardo's. Billy Goat. Who else did you know?"

"You mean, who'd I meet? On the papers? Lots of names. I forget."

"Bullshit," said Karen Kovac softly, still smiling.

"Lady," Mr. Theodore began. His voice was disappointed. The grin was nearly gone.

"You knew newspapermen. You hung around with them. You lent one of them money. Who else did you lend money to? Who else did you hang around with?"

"Hey, I didn't say I hung around with anyone, I just said—"

"You just said you liked to hang around with newspapermen. Who else?" Terry Flynn said.

"Hey." Mr. Theodore looked around the bar filling with people. He seemed disconcerted. "Hey." But the two detectives said nothing.

"I knew lots of guys. The columnist Pete Markk. I knew him. Saw him in the bars."

"You ever lend Markk money?"

"Ha. It'd be the other way around, I think. He's a fucking Finn, you know that,

I thought he was a Polack. He can drink. Man, I'd weigh six hundred pounds, I drink like him. Hates everybody, even me. But he's funny, you know."

"I don't know. You lend him money?"

"Naw. That's one newspaperman you gotta run no tag day for. He's got it all."

"So who you lend money to?"

"I tole you. I don't mix business with pleasure."

"You did with your buddy, Francis Sweeney."

"Francis was different. Maybe I know the guy off and on ten years. A long time. We knew people from the neighborhoods even. My aunt knew his mother when they was both living out to Twenty-fourth and Oakley except his mother moves when she got married to South Shore. That's a small world."

"Old home week," Terry Flynn said. "Enough about the good old days. What about Pete Markk?"

"Markk, I got stiff with him a couple of times, I didn't like his company after a while. He starts on about I'm a dago, you know, you get tired of that shit after a while."

"I wouldn't know, not being a dago,"

Terry Flynn said.

"Aw, fuck. I'm talkin' to you like you're a human being and you're doing a cop. Fuck it. I ain't talking to you no more."

Terry Flynn flushed.

Mr. Theodore turned to the bar.

Flynn stood up, opened his sheepskin jacket, and snapped the cuff on Theodore's right wrist in one practiced movement, pushing behind the big man and slamming his bulk against the bar. It rattled. Two Italian men in suitcoats at a far table stared at the tableau a moment.

"I could take you," Theodore said.

"Maybe. But there's more of us than there are of you."

"You really think that, asshole?" Theodore said softly. "On the cops' best day, we got you surrounded."

"But we got love on our side," Terry Flynn said and snapped the second cuff on Theodore's big left wrist. "The car is down the street, you got a winter coat?"

"No."

"Macho," Karen Kovac said.

"You're a fucking pig too," Theodore said to her.

"That'll cost you," Terry Flynn said.

Which is why Theodore bumped his head severely on the side of the roof of the unmarked car as he was being helped into the backseat. Terry Flynn said later the large man must have slipped on the snowy walk.

17

Another Side of the Story

"You want to talk to me?"

Mr. Theodore stared at the black man and said nothing. He was sitting, cuffed to the chain on the wall, in a straight chair at a plain table in a windowless room.

The black man was L. C. Charles. The initials stood for nothing, he had decided long before; so he was plain L.C. to nearly everyone and Cowboy to intimates (the "cow" coming from Elsie and "cowboy" from the tooled .44 Smith and Wesson with the long barrel he carried in a large holster on his waist). He had worked Homicide and Tactical and now was on detached liaison with the Organized Crime squad inside the

detective division. He was forty-six, his close-cut hair was starting to gray at the temples, and he had a soft, brown face and startling black eyes that glittered lazily.

"He doesn't want to talk to me," L. C. Charles said.

Matt Schmidt grunted. The homicide lieutenant took out a new toothpick and probed his mouth thoughtfully.

"Know what I think? Mr. Theodore is sitting with us for four hours and nobody is going around to the districts looking for him. No lawyers, no runners. Nobody inside Organized Crime knows we got Mr. Theodore."

"That's bullshit, L.C.," Terry Flynn said. "We snatched him right out of the Vernon Park Tap in broad daylight. Everyone knows we got Mr. Theodore and we want to talk to him. But the thing is, nobody knows what it's about. Right, Theodore?"

He did not speak. He stared, bored, at the wall opposite. He would endure. The time would come when they had to let him go.

"Mr. Theodore figures we got to let him go in time. Right, Mr. T.?"

Lazy eyes up, surveying the brown, soft

face, the amazing eyes. Nothing. Theodore glanced away. There was nothing to focus on in the room. The lights were too bright; the voices sounded small in the room.

"Fuck, Flynn," L. C. Charles said at last, throwing down a copy of the *Sun-Times* on the table just to make a loud noise. "Let's charge the motherfucker with something. Your man in the SAO can hold him."

"Fuck you, *tutsone*," Mr. Theodore said at last. It was too much, listening to this one and that one dance with him. "I walk as soon as I make my call."

"He called me a nigger in dago, you hear that?" L. C. Charles said to Terry Flynn.

"You don't have to take that shit," Terry Flynn said. "Hit him with the phone book. I'll go get one. You want the alphabet or the yellow pages?"

The two detectives stared at each other a moment. L. C. Charles grinned at Terry Flynn over the table and the massive head of the prisoner.

Mr. Theodore rumbled: "Assholes. Amateurs. You fucking guys are a riot."

"Maybe I'll just sap him."

"He violated your civil rights, L.C."

Matt Schmidt had said nothing during

191

the banter between the detectives. Now he said, "He really wanted to cooperate with us, Terry."

"He did?"

"Sure. That's why he came in."

Terry Flynn stared at Matt Schmidt.

"Fuck it, lieutenant," Theodore said. "This guy snaps cuffs on me, he bangs me around at the car because I said something to his . . ." He started to say something, looked up at Flynn, and continued, ". . . to the woman. So everyone knows I ain't here because I want to be here."

"But nobody knows about what a pal you were with Sweeney."

"So what? Lots of guys know lots of guys," Theodore said.

"But not a lot of guys know a reporter who owed money and got beat to death and it turns out the guy was a juice man with the Outfit, right?" said L. C. Charles. "That's what you call serendipity fo' da poh-leese."

"Fuck, you couldn't spell it," said Mr. Theodore in his lazy growl. "I wanna make a call."

"Fuck your call and your motherfucking rights," L. C. Charles said. "How much

money you lend your buddy?"

"I didn't lend him nothing."

"That isn't what his widow says," Schmidt interrupted. "She says she remembered your name. On some notes that Sweeney kept. And down at the paper, your name pops up when we go through Sweeney's stuff. Now we're going to start talking to the reporters about you."

"Is that right?"

"That's right," said L. C. Charles.

"Look at me. I'm trembling."

Again, the detectives filed out of the interview room into an adjoining office to talk to each other. It was part of the wearing pattern of interrogation. Periods of threats, questions, wheedling pleas were followed by periods of utter, blank silence in a white-walled windowless room where the prisoner could contemplate the loneliness of the situation. Theodore, of course, was too tough to crack.

"Did he kill Sweeney?" Karen Kovac said.

"I don't know. I don't think so," L. C. Charles replied. "He could have killed him, I mean, Theodore is one very mean sort of person, but I don't know, it doesn't sound

right. I mean, he knew the dude, he was seen with him, eventually we were going to find out about his connection with Sweeney; why would he kill the guy knowing the kind of heat that'd go down?"

"Outfit macho," Terry Flynn said. "Since the jambrones saw *The Godfather*, they're all dressing in pinstripe suits and black shirts again and talking Outfit shit to each other."

They paused for a moment because everyone seemed talked out.

"Leverage," said Matt Schmidt at last. They all stared at him.

"Now we can use Jack Donovan. And the papers."

"How?"

"We've got to get inside Sweeney's life. The paper thinks that policemen shouldn't be harassing newspaper people. Everyone is walking on eggs when we talk to anyone. The paper has got a lawyer dogging our steps when we want to question Clayton. Well, we've got to crack it open. And Mr. Theodore is going to help us."

Terry Flynn stared, blinked, and grinned slowly. He saw it.

Matt Schmidt nodded at him.

Terry Flynn said, "We tell the truth for a

change. That we have found that the dead man might have been involved in paying off a loan shark. Jesus, I love it. And we're trying to get to the bottom of any possible connection between reporters and the Outfit."

"Yeah."

L. C. Charles grinned. "Makes it uncomfortable for Mr. T. for a while. That'd be all right by me. I get bored watching dago funerals with the Sisters." The Sisters were the common inside name for the FBI, picked up from the CIA usage of the late 1960s. The organized-crime unit of the Chicago police department and special crime units from federal agencies made a practice of attending all funerals and weddings among family members of the loose affiliation called the Outfit for the purpose of photographing all participants and harassing them at the same time.

"The only thing we got to do now," Matt Schmidt said slowly, "is get to the newspapers before they can get to us." And that's the way they worked it.

__18_____

New Lead, Sub Story

Two days passed in the depth of the Chicago winter. The mayor of Chicago came to the wake but not the funeral. He participated in a decade of the rosary recited in the funeral home by Father Aloysius MacCarthy of Christ the King parish who had gone to grammar school with Sweeney. There were many mourners, including people who had hated Francis X. Sweeney for years. Mr. Theodore, though freed on bail on charges of loan sharking, did not attend the funeral. He sent a display of white roses without a note.

There were many flowers in Room C of the funeral home on the Southwest Side.

The newspaper sent a wreath and so did the newspaper union and so did colleagues from other papers; there was a wreath from the Chicago Press Club, where Sweeney's name was posted on the delinquent-membership board. He had died owing the club $412, owing the newspaper credit union $2,305, and owing Mr. Theodore $500.

"Hail Mary, full of grace, the Lord is with thee. Blessed art thou amongst women, and blessed is the fruit of thy womb, Jesus," Father MacCarthy said aloud. And the others at the wake, including the mayor, bowed their heads before the casket containing the remains of Francis Sweeney and rumbled:

"Holy Mary, Mother of God, pray for us sinners now, and at the hour of our death. Amen."

The room smelled sickly sweet, full of dying flowers; like a hospital room. Francis Sweeney, his dead hands wrapped around a rosary, rested on a bed of silk. His face was heavily made up, partly to disguise the facial trauma from the blow that broke his skull. The effect was hideous but everyone who grasped the widow's hands and held them said, "He looks so good."

John Hague and a contingent of top exec-

utives from the paper attended all in a bunch, after the prayers were said. Michael Queeney arrived with them but stayed after they left.

He had come to the front of the room as the others did and knelt on the kneeler before the casket and bowed his head over the remains of Francis X. Sweeney. For a long time, he stared down at the face of the dead man. He tried to see the child he had known when he had been a child. He stared at Sweeney's dead face and looked for himself in it, tried to see himself dead, in a coffin, with Sweeney alive, praying over him. He saw nothing finally and felt only a continuing, marvelous confusion.

Jack Donovan, as planned, begged a ride to the North Side from Hague.

And Terry Flynn, as planned, waited outside the home for Michael Queeney to leave. To talk to him. The newspaper was on the defensive and the barriers were down. And a wake is a time that breaks down barriers even more.

Karen Kovac was dining that night with the star columnist of John Hague's paper, Peter Markk. Markk never went to wakes and never rode in airplanes. He was peculiar

in other ways as well, which most people mistook for genius. Markk had been a pal of Mr. Theodore.

Michael Queeney had been a boyhood friend of Francis Sweeney.

And John Hague—no one knew where John Hague stood and what he wanted from the police. Or even from the investigation.

At least they were doing something, Matt Schmidt had said when they talked about the plan. It was going to be an interesting night because at the end of it, when the funeral director turned out the lights in the sweet-smelling room where the remains of Francis X. Sweeney rested in his open coffin, when the widow was home, beyond tears, bone tired, sleeping in her own bed alone as she had so many nights during her marriage to Sweeney, when the city slept a deep winter night and a new storm gathered north of the city, one of the detectives investigating the murder of a reporter would suddenly realize who the killer was.

19

Peter Markk

"What can you tell me?"

"What do you want to know?" He smiled. "About my sex life?"

"No."

"You said you weren't married."

"Not any more."

"You're a cute kid."

Karen Kovac did not smile. The matter was difficult, the most sensitive of the three assignments. Peter Markk was not a friend of the department (as the police would put it). He was widely read, intensely introspective, acerbic. Some people thought he was a brilliant columnist. Some people thought he was merely an asshole. That's the way Terry

Flynn put it when Matt Schmidt and Jack Donovan decided on the assignments that night. The arrest of Mr. Theodore had suddenly put the newspapers—and, subsequently, the rest of the media—on the defensive. It would take another day or two for righteous indignation to reemerge.

They were in the Corona Cafe on Rush Street, at a back table near the white wall at the north end of the big dining room. It was nearly nine; the place was not very busy.

Markk was a tall, angular man with a short nose and dull black eyes and thinning black hair. He wore a thin mustache. He was a chain smoker, his teeth were yellow and small, and his clothes were expensive. He had a vodka martini in front of him that was essentially a glass of vodka with ice cubes. It was the third. They had not ordered dinner yet. And Karen Kovac drank beer.

She wore a blue dress of soft wool with long sleeves and a high buttoned bodice. Terry Flynn called it her nun's dress. She supposed it was.

"What's it like to write five columns a week?" she began carefully. She had thought of six or seven general questions and gone

through three of them. Peter Markk took a long time to answer each question. He enjoyed talking about himself.

"I've done it twenty years," he said thoughtfully, forcing the smoke out of his mouth so that he could replace it with more smoke. "It's just life. It's just part of breathing or waking up or anything." It was the kind of thing he probably had said once on the Johnny Carson show; he wasn't sure.

"I couldn't do that," she said. "I couldn't expose myself like that."

"Sure you could," Peter Markk replied. "People expose themselves all the time." He smiled a satyr's grin. "I bet you've exposed yourself."

She was not charmed by the banter, though Terry Flynn might have said the same sort of thing to her and it would not have mattered. But Terry Flynn, when he first met Karen, had been so tongue-tied that familiarity with her had been as difficult as anything he had tried.

Karen Kovac frowned then. She thought of Terry Flynn and Peter Markk, and she did not want to be here.

"Look, you can't take a line, let it drop. I thought cops were tough."

"It wasn't that. I was thinking of something else."

That annoyed Markk. He expected total attention. He stared at her. "Are cops tough? Even lady cops?"

"No. I don't think they're that much different from anyone else. Except for the physical part," she said. She was being honest and he didn't understand her. "I mean, the physical part gives you an edge. You know you'll draw down on someone. Or go into a basement after someone. Because you've done it. You've been scared but you've done it. So that changes because most people aren't sure what they would do."

"I was at the convention in 'sixty-eight."

"I was in high school," she said.

"Yeah. The cops beat the shit out of a lot of people."

"Yes. I heard about that. I read your columns."

He smiled. "A liberal cop."

"No. Not at all," she said. Quietly. She didn't want to cross him because he seemed dangerous, unpredictable. There was a tension around him that seemed to charge the air of the room. But he suddenly shrugged, smiled:

"You wanna eat?"

"Yes."

They ordered. He recommended a steak. She accepted his order for wine. She felt a little helpless in this place, trapped with some sort of media star.

She knew how Terry Flynn had felt from the beginning of the investigation.

"I'm gonna tell you whatever the fuck you wanna know," he began. "Then we eat and talk and I take you up to a place on Rush. Okay?"

"Okay," she lied.

"Honey, just relax," he said. "I just thought of something. You're not carrying a gun, are you?"

"Yes."

"I mean, now," he said.

"Yes," she said.

"Are you going to shoot me?"

"I hope not," she said.

He lit another cigarette and smiled. "Did you ever shoot anyone?"

"Yes."

"Who?"

"A man."

"What did he do?" The tension was back. She sat very still, her hands folded in front

of her. Karen Kovac did not know how to get out of the question. Perhaps all she could do was answer it and accept the probing of a nightmare she had been trying to put in the back of her mind for two years. She could never completely forget it, not as long as she lived; she had accepted that. But she tried never to speak of it because it reminded her of the terror that had crawled inside her and might someday take her over again.

"He broke my arm. It was in a gangway. It was snowing. He was going to rape me, I think. He had a knife and he was going to kill me."

Peter Markk squinted at her across the smoky table. "What did you do?"

"I shot him."

"Killed him?"

"Yes."

"How did that make you feel?"

"Not good."

"When did this happen?"

"Two years ago."

"You hate men?"

"No."

"You're divorced. You got kids?"

"Yes."

"Your old man pay alimony?" The ques-

205

tions were not soft. He was pushing her and she realized she was going to answer everything.

"Child support."

"Same thing."

"No, Mr. Markk. It is not the same thing." She realized she was talking very precisely, like her Polish grandmother, the words splitting apart like bits of chopped wood, falling into neat piles, all of it clean and precise. Almost rote.

But he smothered her with another smile, mocking and not gentle. He was pulling back into silence. What had Terry Flynn said once? He was a meat eater. That's what Terry Flynn would have called him, one of the urban survivors. Terry divided the known world into meat eaters and fish eaters. The fish eaters, however good and bright, could not survive in the city game. And Terry Flynn always described the terms of the game.

"What's he do? Your old man?"

"He works in advertising."

"A whore."

"No, Mr. Markk."

"Call me Pete."

"He's not a whore. He does what he

does. The way you do."

"I'm a whore then?"

She closed her eyes only for a moment and then opened them. She did not want this. "Mr. Theodore."

"You mentioned his name. Everyone is talking about the Outfit. That's crap, you know. I know it and so does the brass. Newspapermen aren't into the Outfit. But it was clever. *Chicago Today* ran another big story tonight about Jake Lingle, Capone's flunky. Nice. Takes the heat off you guys."

"You think the Brothers of Mecca had something to do with Sweeney's death?"

Markk smiled. "Naw. That's John Hague's paranoia, not mine."

"Why do all of you pursue it?"

"When you're part of a lynch mob, it's better to be in the middle than on the edge. Besides, John Hague pays my bar bill at the moment and he's got a bug up his ass about this one."

"I talked to Mr. Sweeney's widow. She hated his business. You talk with contempt for it. Even Mr. Queeney. I don't understand."

"What don't you understand? Come on, honey, don't shit me. You talk to cops,

don't you? They love being cops, sweeping up garbage that's still warm? Doing the dirty work? My old man was a janitor. He got bitten by rats at least ten times I knew of. Everybody in this world lives on the second floor of a two-flat, you know it? We talk to each other. We la-de-da around like there's no basements, even in our own building. But there is. And there's still gotta be some-body living in the basement. And the janitor may only hang around with other janitors but he doesn't love it, you know. He's not crazy, you know. Being a janitor is shit. Like being a cop." He paused but she made no expression. "Or even a newspaper-man."

He smiled again. His moods seemed so strange to her, nothing in a straight line. How could he live with himself? Karen Kovac thought. He seemed like two men.

"Tell me about Mr. Theodore," she said quietly.

A waiter brought her salad and a plate of cottage cheese for Peter Markk.

"There's not much to tell about him. He's a street character. I bumped into him a few times in the Billy Goat. I think we went out on a bender once, I don't remember. He

talks all that gangster stuff, it's terrific. He wants me to write a column about him."

"Did he say that?"

"He didn't need to. I know when people want me to write a column about them. Half the broads I lay aren't laying me. I could have leprosy and they'd go down on me. They like to rub themselves up against my column."

She waited for a moment. Her voice would not be trustworthy. When she spoke it was cold, quiet. "He talks like a gangster because that's what he is."

"So what?" Markk took a bite of cottage cheese. "That doesn't make him a bad guy."

"It does to me."

"He's no more a juice man than some fucking banker charging you fourteen percent interest to buy a house."

"I don't think like that," she said.

"You can't afford to. You're on one softball team and they're the other team. You gotta believe in this bullshit. I don't."

"Did he lend you money?"

"Are you kidding? I could buy guys like him all day."

"Then why did you hang around with him?"

"I didn't. He talks to me in a bar. One night when I'm not getting laid, he wants to take me to a couple of greaseball joints, so I go with him. He's a star fucker, he's got a star fucker's mentality. That is not the same as hanging around with him. Would you like to go to bed with me?"

"No."

"Even if I wrote a column about what a great cop you are?" Smiling but without humor.

"No."

"Why not?" The smile faded. "You don't like me, right?"

"I don't know if I like you or not."

"Sure you do. People make judgments right away. You like someone or you don't. I try to make it easier for them."

"Yes. By putting on a little show," she said. "You say, 'This is the worst I can be.' And people have to accept it and then you have contempt for them for taking it because it means they are weak or you have something they want so badly they can be humiliated."

"Like you, honey."

"Yes. But I deal with people like you all the time. I get used to it. Mr. Theodore.

You. Garbage. As you said."

He threw the plate of cottage cheese at her. Part of it struck her dress.

She sat still for a moment.

There were five diners in the room. A waiter hurried toward the table.

Karen Kovac wiped the remains of the cottage cheese from her dress. She dipped her napkin in the water glass and wiped at the spot. It was absurd, she thought. If she were more angry, she would have known what to do. But she felt sad.

When she had finished, she put down her napkin. The waiter hovered a little distance from the table, uncertain about what to do. The other diners continued to stare.

"What are you going to do?" Karen Kovac said.

"Me? I just did it."

"I am a police officer," she said in the same quiet voice. "I can arrest you for assaulting an officer. I am also on official business, investigating a murder. You refuse to answer questions, you assault me."

"You called me garbage."

"Did I?"

"Okay. I see. You going to arrest me?"

"Do you want me to?"

Her voice was still very even, very clear, cold as a well in winter.

"No," he said at last, turning his eyes to the table.

"Will you answer my questions?"

"Yes."

"Who knew Mr. Theodore? At the paper?"

"Me." Slowly, reluctantly, the bad boy trying to start fresh. "Sweeney knew him, always hung around with him. I know he lent Sweeney money."

"Did he threaten Sweeney? About payment?"

"Yeah. Once in the Billy Goat, Sweeney said he had to go, he said the Lavender Goon was looking for him. I figure he meant Theodore."

"So you think this meant that Theodore was threatening him?"

"Maybe. I did at the time."

"When was this?"

"Couple of months ago."

"Who else on the paper knew Theodore?"

"A copy editor named Tillman. Tillman drank in the Goat after his shift, after the home delivery, around eleven at night."

"Anyone else?"

"No one I can think of who was as close as Sweeney."

"Did Sweeney ever say Mr. Theodore hurt him? Hit him or specifically threatened him?"

Markk frowned, lit another cigarette. "No."

"And who else might not like Sweeney?"

"Nobody much likes anyone. It's the nature of the business. Editors don't like reporters, reporters don't like copyreaders, copyreaders don't like printers. It's called creative tension."

"Who else doesn't like Sweeney enough to kill him?"

"That's the sixty-four-dollar question, isn't it?"

"You?"

Markk stared at her through the smoke he was creating. "Sweeney is a fly in the ointment of life as far as I'm concerned. I've forgotten him already. He was of passing interest to me. Find someone else, honey."

"We could still finish this in headquarters," she said evenly. "You can call me Karen Kovac. That's my name."

"Liberated, huh? Give someone a gun and right away they think they're better

than other people."

"Anyone who breathes is better than you."

Markk's face flushed again but he did not move.

"You seem easily excited to violence. Especially against people you perceive to be . . . less than you. Someone like Sweeney. Sweeney was a middle-aged man, fat, he might have been easy to beat up. Didn't you get into a fight in a tavern three years ago on North Avenue and beat up a drunkard?"

"Yeah." Markk stubbed out the cigarette. "It was nollied. I settled with him. I worked a couple of months free. But I was drunk myself."

"Why would you want Sweeney to die?"

"Sweeney? Dead or alive made no difference to me. Sweeney was wallpaper as far as I was concerned."

Karen Kovac stared at him for a long time.

Markk stubbed out another cigarette. The waiter brought steaks. He seemed wary of both of them. "Is everything all right?"

"Yeah, yeah," said Markk.

But neither touched the food for a long

moment. Then Markk reached for a knife.

"I like the steak you get here," he said inanely to her. And she understood. He was afraid of her. It was all right then.

She put down her napkin and got up. The slightly damp spot on her dress was scarcely visible.

"Hey, are you going? Come on, sid-down."

"No, Mr. Markk. The interview is over for now," Karen Kovac said. She stared at him and then smiled slowly.

"You like steak, Mr. Markk," Karen Kovac said. "But I don't think you're a meat eater at all."

20

John Hague

The Lincoln purred along the Stevenson Expressway, curving across the Southwest Side toward the twinkling lights of the Loop. The cloudy winter sky was colored red by the lights of the city thrown into the atmosphere. There were no stars.

John Hague curled in a corner of the stretch limousine, his feet propped on a jump seat turned into a temporary stool. He seemed smaller than he was. Everything inside the car created an illusion that distorted size, even as the Loop seen through the car windows seemed to be uprooted, floating above the ground, without base. Jack Donovan sat as close to him as he thought

John Hague would stand.

Hague's shirt was rumpled, his tie was wrinkled. His whole manner seemed tired, defeated. It too was an illusion. People who knew John Hague—or thought they did—said it was a physical ruse, part of a daily phenomenon when, at the end of the cycle of work, he was so used up and exhausted that it seemed he was fit for nothing but a long sleep and quiet days ahead. In fact, after three or four hours of sleep, he would be up before dawn, restlessly prowling the corridors of his newspaper (he had an apartment a few blocks away in the John Hancock Center), reading the competition, reading the wire reports clattering out news from the world, selectively reading his other newspapers flown in daily. He had been in Chicago for a week, his longest period in the town. His usual base was New York, where he also owned a paper.

"What are we going to talk about?" John Hague said without preliminaries in his curious, efficient, and clipped Canadian accent, flat as the Albertan wheatlands.

"About who killed Francis Sweeney."

"I didn't know you were a policeman as well as a prosecutor."

217

"I'm not. But this whole special team was your idea, so don't be surprised by what turns out."

"I wouldn't take shit like that from my editor," John Hague said in a quiet, precise voice.

"But I don't work for you."

"Your boss hasn't done a very good job so far in finding out who killed my reporter," John Hague said. His chin was firm, the gray eyes glittering. A glass partition divided the driver from the two men in the back of the long black car.

Jack Donovan understood; Hague was reminding him that he worked for Bud Halligan but Halligan, in a sense, was now working for John Hague. The understanding did not anger Donovan. It was a threat, of course; but because it was delivered with such pale, uninflected and even soft words, it seemed much more virulent.

"Your paper doesn't seem interested in finding out who killed Francis Sweeney."

The statement hung in the still air a moment.

"Go ahead. You've got ten minutes before I get home."

"It is wrongheaded," Jack Donovan said. "You've identified the killer without any evidence and blindly driven the police to make arrests without any evidence. You don't really seem to care who killed Sweeney as long as you can name a killer. A killer to fit in with one of your editorial theories."

"Did your boss, your Mr. Halligan, send you to insult me?"

"No. But you're not stupid, Mr. Hague. Think about it."

Hague blinked. "Where do you come from? What's your background?"

"Why?"

"Because I have ten . . . make it nine minutes to understand something about you, decide about you. If it were morning and you were looking for a job, I could size you up in thirty seconds. That's the secret, Donovan. You have to go with your instincts in my position but you've got to make sure your instincts are right."

"What do your instincts tell you about what I've just said?"

John Hague said flatly, "You might have something there. So tell me who you are."

"South Side Irish."

"What does that mean?"

"You've got to understand the city. It's Queens Irish or Boston Southie."

"Okay. That's good. That frames it."

"I was a cop once."

"And you moved up."

"Not necessarily."

"Go on. You're a barrister . . . lawyer, you think you're better than you were or you wouldn't have changed jobs."

"No," Jack Donovan said.

"Then why change?"

"I thought there was something more to understand."

"About what?"

"About what it was all about."

"And is there?"

"No. It's just the other side of the moon. It still doesn't tell you everything."

"Good. You married?"

"Yes."

"Your wife work?"

"I don't know. She's been missing for three years."

"Kids?"

"Two."

"Okay. I won't ask any more. Why do you want to talk to me?"

"Maybe you know who killed Francis Sweeney."

John Hague stared at him and smiled. "Jack. I'll call you Jack, you call me Mr. Hague, okay? Jack, you want to know something? Tonight is the first night in my life I've ever laid eyes on Francis Sweeney. In his coffin."

"Is that right?"

"Do you know how many newspapers I own?"

"I have some idea."

"I know people through the people I hire to run my papers and through reading my papers. I'm not God."

"That's comforting to the rest of us."

John Hague grinned. "Tough guy, eh, Jack?"

But Donovan did not smile. "Why did you have Sweeney writing about the Brothers of Mecca? And why them?"

"What do you mean?"

"You don't know a thing about Chicago."

"I told you, Jack, you hire people, size them up, let them run the thing. The paper I run in New York is nothing like the paper in Chicago. Different markets, different goals."

"What's your goal? I mean, here?"

"Make money, Jack." Grinned. "That's what it's about, Jack."

"There are easier ways of doing it."

"Right, Jack. I like that, you see right through it. My father—your father alive?"

"No."

"What'd he do?"

"He worked for the CTA."

"Doing what?"

"Started as a motorman. He was from the old country."

"Good, Jack. Son of an immigrant. Same with my father. He had the bad sense to become a farmer in Alberta province, he couldn't grow a beard up there. Died. Now what do you think I want to do? Same as you, Jack. Rub their noses in it. Is that why you became a cop?"

"No."

"Why?"

"I didn't want to be a motorman."

"Okay, Jack, bullshit me but just don't bullshit yourself too much. I own newspapers, which makes me a lot more important than being a rich man. I'm rich but the world is full of rich people, don't let the Communists kid you about it. But it doesn't

have a lot of important people. I'm important, Jack. I count. I can put your Mr. Bud Halligan through a hoop wearing a tutu and he'll thank me for it afterward."

"So you like to push people around."

"I like to push around people who push around people. Like the Mecca gang. Dopers, terrorists, extortionists, bad people. The blacks are hopeless, Jack, you know it and so do I. They've been put on the dole too long in this country, just like the free grain they gave the mob in Rome. There are always too many urban poor and they lose their dignity and self-respect faster than the rural poor. We've corrupted the blacks, they've lost their dignity and replaced it with their demand for rights. Well, this demand has become perverted. We've got presidential candidates kissing the black asses of racists and rhetorical fascists simply because white people have become afraid of the mob. Don't rock the boat. Give them free grain. Or food stamps. Buy them off, keep them quiet, while we get on with our business of running an empire. It won't work, Jack. Didn't in Rome, won't work here. I want people to stand up to these black bully boys. They're nothing but fas-

cists of a different color."

"All the blacks are niggers, Hague?"

"Naw, Jack, don't get my goat. But we're talking about a whole population here, not those who got out of it."

"You're a racist, Hague."

John Hague laughed. "Good, Jack. Now let me give you the other side of the argument. I want to go after the Mecca group because they are a cancer in the black population, they victimize black people, they are the living symbol of the sort of racism we tolerate. We do nothing about black gangs like the Meccas because the black gangs do not threaten the white majority and because nobody cares what goes on in the ghetto. Do you like that argument?"

Jack Donovan did not speak.

"You see, Jack, I can give it to you either way—the niggers have to be rooted out and kept down, or the blacks need equal protection under the law. Now, what do I really feel? It's none of your business. Everyone writes about me, about bad John Hague, the sleaze merchant, and nobody understands a damned thing about me or about what I really think because I won't tell them. I don't owe it to some prissy cunt

with the *Wall Street Journal* who wants a big interview so she can cut me to ribbons, and I don't owe it to you."

"You're wrong, Hague." Softly. "You do owe it," Jack Donovan said. "A man was killed and I want to understand why you don't want us to find his killer."

"So you cut through everything I've just said and you go back to the same question. We've got five minutes left, Jack. Don't be tiresome."

"Who picked Sweeney to write about the Mecca gang? Who suggested a campaign against them?"

"My M.E., Queeney. It's a good crusade. It's flagging a bit but Sweeney's murder has perked up interest."

"Sweeney is just a circulation builder."

"Sweeney isn't anything. He's dead. I gave his widow a check for twenty-five thousand dollars at the wake."

Jack Donovan blinked.

"In addition to Sweeney's life insurance and all that. Not bad, eh, Jack? Do you think I should do a story about myself?"

"No."

"No, neither do I. Charity speaks loudest when it is silent."

225

"Is the Outfit involved in your paper?"

"You mean the crime syndicate? Of course," John Hague said.

Jack Donovan stared at him.

"Jack, the crime syndicate is involved in everything. They're in unions, and newspapers have unions and I suppose the syndicate decides if my papers get on the street; I don't really know. If you mean involved in the way you cops put out that silly story about a loan shark named . . ."

"Theodore."

"Yes. Nice ploy. That takes the heat off. That gets you a ride downtown with me."

"Why do you want the heat when all it does is screw up a murder investigation?"

"Because he was my reporter and I won't let my reporters get killed. It's that simple. And if I have to turn the screws up, I'll do it."

"But maybe your reporter didn't get killed because of what he was writing."

"And maybe he did. Maybe you people just want us to go away so you can file this case in the dead-letter office or whatever you have."

"Most killers know their victims."

"And sometimes they don't."

"Someone on your newspaper killed Sweeney," Jack Donovan said. He heard his own voice as though listening to someone else.

John Hague said mildly, "That's an interesting idea. A drunk reporter found dead in an alley, police alter evidence to hide the real killers because it would bring too much heat into the city to say that a bunch of black racist terrorists had killed a white man and threatened a black man—both of whom worked for me—"

"They victimize their own. You said it."

"But did I believe it?" Again, the annoying grin. Crumpled in the corner of the backseat, John Hague grinned like a gremlin in the half-darkness. His face moved in and out of shadows under the passing streetlamps. "Let's say they start with one and then get the other. Let's say they're after Clayton now."

"Desmond Clayton is in a bad position," Jack Donovan said.

"And so are you. And your special team or whatever it is. And Mr. Bud Halligan, your boss."

"Did Clayton and Sweeney get along?"

"I wouldn't know that. Ask one of my

editors. Your detectives have access to our office."

"Why don't you want us to find the killer?" Jack Donovan said.

"Thank God we're there. You're boring, Jack."

The big car pulled up at the residential entrance of the one-hundred-story Hancock building off Michigan Avenue. The wind whipped fiercely around the exposed steelwork. John Hague reached for the door handle and spoke to the driver. "Take him wherever he wants to go, Kevin." He looked at Jack and smiled again.

"Piece of advice, Jack boy, good advice because I'm a rich man and I have good instincts."

Donovan stared at him.

"Never trust a man who has no secrets."

__21__

The Man Within

They ended up in a small bar on the Southeast Side just beyond the South Shore neighborhood, not far from the shuttered South Works of U.S. Steel.

The neighborhood was black and Mexican with slivers of white residents remaining. The different racial and ethnic groupings drank in their own bars. This place was mostly white. Jim and George had inherited the place from their father, a Greek immigrant.

"Me and Francis got drunk in here once. Maybe more than once," said Michael Queeney.

The two men progressed slowly across

the South Side over three hours. What had begun as an interview had become a conversation between Sergeant Terry Flynn and Michael Queeney.

Flynn's eyes were glittering as much as Queeney's. Flynn drank tap beer. Queeney drank from a bottle, and a shot of whisky intervened from time to time.

The place was like two thousand other neighborhood taverns strung across the city, warm against the brutal darkness of winter, full of reddish glows from beer signs, full of illusions for a winter night of unending darkness. It was a weekday night in dull January. The streets were littered with piles of dirty snow. There was a sort of desperate gaiety inside the tavern. Beyond the double doors was the wind and dark and a smell of snow in the air.

"I drink down here. Get away from Hague's people. None of those assholes even know there's a South Side. Come down here to be Michael Queeney and not the guy watching my ass all the time."

Flynn nodded. He understood. He thought he understood everything.

"It gets rough," Terry Flynn said.

"What?"

"Working for new bosses. I know about that. When I transferred out of Tac to the Special Squad. Working for Matt Schmidt the first time. He turned out to be all right."

"My mother's still alive," said Michael Queeney, completing the non sequitur. "Eighty-three. I got to watch her, I try to get to her house a couple of times a week. My sister's married, five kids, no time to see the old lady. Well, she was always a bitch, my sister. Eighty-three, you imagine it, and she still goes to mass on Sunday. I don't think I'm going to make eighty-three. Hell, who cares? I don't care."

"Sweeney didn't care. From everything you said about him. From everything everyone else said about him."

"Cared a lot. Francis. He cared too fucking much about this magic show we put on every day."

"Magic show. That's what it is?"

"What do you think it is? You believe in newspapers? Touching if you do. I bet you believe in Santa Claus."

"Why did Sweeney care too much?"

"I don't know what you're talking about."

"Sweeney cared too much," said Terry Flynn. "You said it, not me."

"This was a great city," said Queeney, his eyes clouding. "Could ride a fucking streetcar to any neighborhood. When I was a kid, used to clean up down at Comiskey Park after the game so they'd give me a pass to the next game. Me and Sweeney. We took the El all over the city. I remember we hitched on a freight once pulling out of Dearborn station, Jesus Christ, we were halfway to Mississippi before it stopped. You know what we did? Sweeney stole a car. We dropped it in the neighborhood, went home, my father beat the shit out of me, wanted to know where I had been. I think the cop knew. Barney worked the neighborhood then. Back when they had cops on the beat. Now nobody gives a shit." His voice altered suddenly, doing an imitation of an urban black accent with its speeded-up patter and drawn-out vowels: "Shee-it, now nobody see the jiveass mu'fucking poh-leese ossifer on de beat, you know, da people, dey runs they own neigh-borhoods theyself, don't want no Barney. Don't wan' no Michael Queeney poking his jiveass honkie ass into shit where it don' belongs."

Flynn was nodding, listening, still trying

232

to focus. What was he seeing? In the noise of the small tavern, he thought he was beginning to see it but it was lost in the smoke, in the presence of Queeney so close to him. He tried something else: "How's Sweeney's wife doing?"

"Better. You know, I used to go out with Maureen. I told you that."

"Yeah. We know that."

"Poor kid."

"She picked the wrong guy."

"What?"

"She picked the wrong guy," said Terry Flynn. "Didn't she?"

"Fuck no. Sweeney ended up . . . not good. But Francis was a good man. Really a good man. You don't bad-mouth Francis to me. I stuck my neck out for him a lot of times."

"Like on the Mecca investigation."

"Yeah. I almost got it chopped off."

"Did Clayton make up the stories?"

Queeney blinked through his wireless spectacles at the big policeman next to him. "No. I tried to follow through on that."

"You talked to Clayton."

"Yeah."

"That's follow-through?"

233

"Jesus Christ, who elected you to the National News Council? You go with your reporters, you gotta believe them or the whole thing breaks down."

"I wouldn't know about newspapers," Flynn said.

"Is that right?"

"Or about magic shows," added Flynn.

"Now you're talking like an asshole."

"Here's my problem, Michael," said Terry Flynn in a sweet, reasonable tone of voice. "I got a bunch of guys who might have killed Sweeney or might not have killed him.

"I got your ordinary street mugger, some guy sees this drunk in the alley one night and rolls him and kills him. I like that one from the beginning. It's reasonable. It does happen, even in wonderful Chicago.

"But being a policeman, you got to sift through the clues, as we call them in the Ace Crimefighting School. So what do I have? I have Peter Markk, who has a long hard-on for Sweeney. I have Clayton, who is ambitious and is told by his close buddy on the investigation of the Mecca people that Clayton made up his whole story. I got you, his buddy, who admits that Sweeney threat-

ens you and Markk and fifty other people, it seems, into telling dark and dirty newspaper secrets to the waiting world. And then I even got John Hague, who is not Mr. Nice Guy in the business world. He wants to have someone hit, hell, I figure those guys can get anyone to hit anyone. But I want to tell you, Michael, I don't like that last scenario at all. Sweeney couldn't hurt Hague. He was a gnat."

"And you got the Outfit guy, Mr. Theodore," said Michael Queeney. Someone had played the jukebox. The place was full of noise, shouts, even laughter above the music. But between Queeney and Flynn at that moment, frozen at the bar, there was a silence that blotted out all the other sounds.

Finally Flynn spoke. "Mr. Theodore is not above busting the odd kneecap, but the thing you gotta know about juice is that the collector wants the money, starting with the juice. Dead men don't pay. And nobody wants a dead reporter. In fact, a dead reporter doesn't really benefit anyone in this deal. Not Hague. Not Markk, whose dirty secrets about beating up ladies come out of the closet. Not anyone, except you and Clayton."

235

"Me and Clayton?"

"That's it, unless of course it turns out to be just a street mugger that we'll probably never catch anyway."

Queeney waited a moment and then smiled. He poured a drink and banged his bottle of Old Style on the bar. He ordered another for himself and the detective. "Have a shot," Queeney said.

"Sure," said Sergeant Terry Flynn, who had scarcely moved. His eyes never left Queeney's face.

"Cheers," said Queeney, draining the shot of Red Label.

"Whatever," answered Flynn, repeating the gesture.

"I hated to see him in the coffin," said Queeney. "I hated it. You know somebody all your life, you grow up with him, you fuck around with him, you get old with him, and then he's there, not even him, just a corpse, another stiff and you get so used to shutting out the image of corpses, making bad jokes about tragedies . . . and there he is."

"You and Clayton," said Terry Flynn. "And it was you." His voice sounded odd and detached and very calm.

236

God, Terry Flynn thought suddenly, a thought sobering him like a dash of cold water. That was it.

"The death threats. To Sweeney, Clayton. We've got the transcript," said Terry Flynn, still in a calm, trancelike voice.

Queeney said nothing for a long moment but stared at the detective with pure hatred.

"You, Queeney. You son of a bitch. It was you. The fucking ringmaster of the circus, the star of the magic show."

"What are you talking about? You're drunk," Michael Queeney finally said.

"No, asshole. You're drunk. You're the one, the jiveass mu'fucker." Flynn had lapsed into his own parody of black urban speech patterns. Most of the policemen who worked the streets could imitate black patter fairly well. Their ears had been trained through years of working in the ghetto.

And a few old street reporters. Like the kid from the South Side named Michael Queeney.

"You did it to yourself," said Terry Flynn with amazement. It had been there all the time, in plain sight. "You set up the thing with death threats after the series started."

237

"And waited six weeks to kill Sweeney? Brilliant."

"No. You never intended to kill anyone. It was a way of juicing up the series. You had to win some recognition for it. You'd sold it to Hague's people as your project, to show how valuable you were to them in Chicago. You knew the city, you could rap with the shines. So you put this guy Clayton on the streets and he comes up with the story you wanted. Maybe it's true and maybe it isn't, though Sweeney didn't like it and that bothered you a lot. But what really made you kill him? You were his buddy."

Queeney's voice was cold. "You tell me, buddy. You tell me, you're the fucking Sherlock on this one. You don't know shit, you're fishing, you're gonna be walking a beat in Pilsen busting Mexicans before I get finished with you."

"Oh, fuck, don't do that tough shit with me, I heard all the South Side bullshit for years. But I heard that other shit. You were so clever to call yourself when your machine was on, taking the recording of the call. You do a good spade, Michael, but it needs work."

"You got shit."

238

"I got shit, shithead?" Flynn exploded, pushing him. "I got a tape recording with your fucking voice on it. There's voice prints, all kinds of shit you can do. And the afternoon Sweeney falls apart in front of you and Peter Markk and the Hague people, you know you got to fire him to hang onto your own job and then Sweeney, what's Sweeney gonna do? Blow the investigation? Go to one of those fucking hippie papers and tell them that the big investigation of the Mecca religion was just a bunch of jive? You said it yourself: Hague and his crowd didn't know their way around the block in this town. You put it over on them. But why did you kill him? You were his friend, Michael; you shouldn't have killed your friend."

Queeney stared at him for a long time.

"He was my friend."

Flynn waited.

"We were the same person."

And Flynn thought of the man in Fiji who was just like him.

"He hurt so much," said Michael Queeney. "He hated himself so much."

"Yeah," said Flynn at last.

"What are you gonna do?"

"You want to make a statement?"

"I got nothing to say," said Queeney. His face took on the heavy look of an aggressor before the battle. He pushed Flynn's arm as if to shove him away. "You really don't have me."

"Don't believe that. Maybe not today or tomorrow, but I'm just a cop and I knock on doors and talk to people. Cop stuff, Michael, just keep dogging it, keep pushing it, keep asking the questions. I've just started. I'll talk to Maureen again, and then I'm going through the staff again. And we're going to talk to Mr. Hague tomorrow and we aren't going to let up on it."

"You bring a lot of heat on yourself."

"Well, that's the way it goes," said Flynn. "Maybe we wouldn't push it this hard for some cheap murder on the West Side but this is a newspaper murder, a reporter got killed, it's the story on page one. I'm gonna get you, Michael. I like you, you're a good drinker, I even understand you and why you did it. But I'm gonna get you."

"Why?"

"Because you can't murder people, even to put them out of their pain, even if you say you love them. You can't murder

people because you can't decide those things, Michael, you know that. It doesn't work that way."

"What are you going to do?" he asked again, inanely, trying to focus. His eyes were red, and there was a mean growl in his voice. It was the voice of a bully.

"Aw, shit," Terry Flynn said. He turned just a fraction. He really did not expect what happened next.

Queeney pulled Flynn's pistol from his clip on the side of his belt.

Queeney cocked the revolver and pointed it at Terry Flynn.

"Jesus Christ," said Terry Flynn. And then he thought: They'll get him anyway now. But what about the guy in Fiji? Does he die now too? Is that the way it works?

The bar was so still that it might have been a photograph.

"I loved him."

"Give me the pistol. Easy. Uncock it."

"No," said Michael Queeney, raising it chest high, holding it unsteadily.

Flynn glanced to his left. The bar was too crowded. If he jumped for it, it would go off. Someone would die.

"Step back," said Queeney.

Flynn took a step back.

"Another."

"Give me the pistol. You don't want to do this."

"What am I doing?" asked Michael Queeney, the trace of a smile on his lips. "What do you think I'm doing?"

Flynn did not speak. It was so stupid, he thought. Matt will never forgive me for getting killed like this.

"Don't forget my mother," said Michael Queeney. "Drop in on her."

Flynn stared, his eyes wide.

And Michael Queeney put the muzzle of the .357 Colt Python in his mouth and awkwardly pulled the trigger and blew his brains out on the bar behind him.

22

Why Did You Come Back?

Terry Flynn was late getting into the squad room the next morning. There was no hurry. First he saw the old woman who was Michael Queeney's mother and then he visited Maureen Sweeney and by the time he got into the office, it was nearly eleven. They were all waiting for him.

Including Sid Margolies, who was sitting at his old desk. Margolies looked as though he had the beginnings of a tan.

It was snowing.

Forty-four inches of snow had fallen this winter in the city, which was normal according to the man on the radio. Six more inches were expected tonight and early

243

the next morning.

Matt Schmidt and Karen Kovac waited at their desks. Terry Flynn did not speak to any of them as he took off his jacket. Just then, Jack Donovan from the state's attorney's office entered the small room with a half-dozen cups of coffee in plastic containers. They had all shared turns as gofers for the coffee while they waited for Terry Flynn.

"Police convention?" said Terry Flynn. He hung his dirty sheepskin jacket on the peg in the wall and looked around. And then he noticed it.

"Where's the lamp? What happened to the lamp?"

"Someone took it overnight," Karen Kovac said. "We're down to one now."

Another silence. They all stared at him.

"Cops are thieves when it comes down to it," said Terry Flynn. "Except they're dumb. They steal trash."

"Hello," said Sid Margolies, who looked worried. He pulled at his nose in a nervous gesture. "I'm back."

"Why?" said Terry Flynn.

"Because I couldn't stand it."

"Three weeks you were gone."

"It was long enough."

"I'd never come back," Terry Flynn said. He stared out the dirty window at the snow falling. "Jesus Christ, I hate this fucking city, I hate this fucking winter."

"Tell me about Queeney," said Matt Schmidt in a soft voice.

"It was not my proudest moment," said Flynn. "I never thought he was going to grab for my piece. I think I thought he might just fall off a bridge somewhere. Then I thought, for a while, that he was going to kill me and that you would have been mad at me because I was so stupid to let him have my piece."

Karen Kovac became very pale. Terry Flynn seemed distracted as he spoke.

"All the bullshit we went through," said Flynn at last. "It didn't mean anything. Did it mean that the Mecca Brothers are the good guys? Scum. Did it mean that Clayton didn't make up his story? It doesn't matter. Queeney put his pal Sweeney out of his misery and then put himself out of his own misery. Christ, I feel so fucking dirty I washed myself twice this morning and the stink is still on me. It was right there, Matt. He hid it in plain sight. He wanted us to

245

catch him and we weren't fast enough. I should have figured it out earlier."

"Except we were all jumping through the media hoops," said Jack Donovan.

"Crazy way to run a justice system, isn't it?" said Terry Flynn, grinning but not meaning it. "I kept wondering if the guy in Fiji was going to have to die just because I died. Do you think that's why healthy guys suddenly have heart attacks? Their guy in Fiji dies and they have to die too."

"What is this about Fiji?" said Sid Margolies. "I came back to escape craziness. People out there are all crazy."

"Yeah." Terry Flynn paused, pulled out a Lucky Strike, and lit it. "And we're all the sane ones. Live in an arctic climate. Terrific. Shines against the white guys. Everything is okay if you understand that. Terrific."

"I hated it," said Sid Margolies. "I went into the restaurant by the motel the first morning in California. I asked for a BLT on toast. They bring it. Nice. You know what they bring on the side? Tomato. And more lettuce. A little salad with an avocado. On the side. I got a BLT plus I got another BLT without bacon on the side. I knew

then I made a mistake but I stood for it for three weeks. It took me three weeks to admit it."

"So you come back and you're a garbageman again," said Terry Flynn. "You're so wrong, Sid. Get the fuck out while you got the chance."

And nobody could say anything to that.

23

The Man in Fiji

On a January day, they walked along the edge of the frozen lake in Lincoln Park. The wind was light, the trees were outlined in ice, bent against the gray sky. The ice in the lake reached out nearly two miles and then it was open water, the arctic sea extending to the horizon. Lake Michigan steamed in the clear air, the warmer water kissing the light wind brushing above the surface. On the line of the horizon, a lake freighter churned slowly south from the more frozen north.

Terry Flynn had taken her to Lincoln Park Zoo. They had thrown marshmallows at the polar bears restless in their small out-

door cages. They had bought hot dogs at the stand near the Cafe Brauer and ate them as they strolled along. Squirrels scampered endlessly across the frozen crust of the park, storing away against a winter that had long since arrived. Joggers in the park huffed their way along the cinder path that wound down from Hollywood beach on the far North Side to North Avenue. It was so cold that it felt good to them; their faces were as flushed as children's. Karen Kovac's blue eyes were bright and shining in the wind, in the exertion of the walk. They both wore wool watch caps pulled down over their ears, the usual uniform of the winter pedestrian in Chicago, regardless of class or race.

"February tomorrow. Six more months of winter. The groundhog is going to see his shadow and blow his own head off." Terry Flynn frowned at the image. He could not shake the sensation of death that had chilled in the past ten days. "Is it good or bad, seeing his shadow? I forget?"

She smiled. "You're so athletic. Hot dogs in the park in the middle of winter. After this, we go to your place and take all our clothes off and take a shower together."

"Yes. It's the only thing I like about this new save-energy crap," said Terry Flynn. "Getting a day off for a little nookie with my gookie."

"God. You really wish I were Oriental."

"Well, you are, sort of. I mean, you're a Polack. You're a thousand miles east of Ireland, which puts you somewhere near Bangkok, doesn't it?"

She smiled again. "You're so ignorant sometimes, I wonder if it really is an act."

"Did I ever lie to you? Did I ever tell you I was smart? I told you I had a twelve-inch dong and that's all. It's the direct approach."

"You lied that time."

"God, this is better than sex over the phone. Do you think we're sufficiently frozen now? Do you think we can go home?" asked Terry Flynn.

They began to cross the park, their boots breaking the glazed crust of ice above the snow. "You could take a picture of this," Karen Kovac said. "The lakefront, the Loop buildings, the park. It would look good on a postcard."

"An illusion," said Terry Flynn, and Karen knew he was thinking about Michael

Queeney again, about the night Queeney took Terry Flynn's gun and blew the top of his head off in a bar on the South Side.

"Do you still see Queeney's mother?" she asked, her arm in his.

"Yes. They're taking her out of her house and putting her in a nursing home. That's the daughter, the one with five kids. I hope the bitch lives long enough to have her kids shove her in a nursing home. Well. I suppose I don't blame her but the old lady is okay the way she is, where she is. Nobody leaves nobody alone anymore. The neighborhood is bad now too and the daughter gets worried."

"Black."

"Sure, what else do we mean when we say bad anymore? Like Jack Donovan said, talking about John Hague. Nobody can figure the guy out because he's got the rest of us figured out. I understand that, I think. Mirrors and illusions."

"That's pretty deep talk for a certified dummy who doesn't have anything going for him except the size of his pecker," said Karen Kovac.

"God, I love it when broads talk dirty,"

Terry Flynn said. They walked in silence a while. "John Hague holds up the paper every morning like a mirror and we see what we want to see in it. We see ourselves."

"No," Karen Kovac said. "I don't believe that. It's a newspaper is all. Sometimes it gets the facts right and sometimes it doesn't and that's all it is."

"I won't argue with you."

"You better not. I'm a sworn officer and I have full arrest powers."

"Hey, so am I, come to think of it. But I'm on top, I'm a sergeant and you're a peasant."

"You weren't on top last time," she said.

"There you go again. I never knew Polish girls were so horny. I would've gone with them earlier."

"Maybe they're not all like me," said Karen Kovac.

"No. I suppose not." He kissed her nose, which was bright red in the cold. "I love you."

No, she thought. The words were too heavy for so fragile an idea. And then she smiled. He had kissed her nose when he said it. Perhaps that made it easier. "I'd kiss you back but it's too cold," she said.

"I'm afraid our mouths would stick together."

"Only if you have steel teeth," Terry Flynn said.

They crossed Clark Street against the lights and Terry Flynn popped open the door of his Ford. He reached across and popped the lock on her door. She slid inside. The vinyl seat was cold, and she shivered.

He turned the ignition and the car whirred once, twice, and then coughed into life for a lingering moment, and then died.

Flynn said the ritual curse words, turned the ignition again, and this time the engine caught, sputtering, and then stronger. He waited a moment for it to warm up. "Next time around, I'm going to live in Fiji," he said.

"You still think about that."

"The man in Fiji? Yeah. Not serious but I think about it sometimes. It would be a nice way of seeing the world, seeing all the goofy things that happen. We're just mirrors of something happening somewhere else."

"The man in Fiji who has your looks and your fingerprints," she said slowly.

"Maybe he's a beachcomber or a banker. Maybe he drives a cab. I suppose they got cabs in Fiji."

"And if you had died that night in the bar—"

"No. I don't really believe that. But I believe about Queeney. That he was inside his pal. That he was suffering for him even while he was saving his own ass. He wanted that award to make Hague look kindly on him. Hell, maybe to get another job somewhere else. He faked those death threats to goose up the interest in the story. He didn't even care if the story was a fake as long as no one talked about it. And yet he brought in Sweeney to write the story. It turns out that Sweeney might have been the only guy with any integrity. And he was no prize."

She shook her head. "Get out of here, Terry. It's too cold in your car."

"Ah, but it makes all the warm loving later that much better."

And Terry Flynn pulled out of the parking space on the street. The tires climbed the hump of ice and packed snow between the space and the roadway and turned right at the corner and right again onto Lincoln Avenue, going northwest away from the

heart of the city.

Flynn turned down Lill Street and pulled in front of his building. The street was nearly deserted because it was the middle of a work day and most of the people who lived in the area either did not have cars or used them in their jobs. There were no children on the street and only a few families. Most of the people who lived on Lill were like Flynn. Alone.

When they got inside the apartment, Terry Flynn said: "See. Even as I promised you, my little Polish cupcake. Steam heat."

"Mr. Wonderful," she said. They took off their coats and threw them on the bed. "We may need that bed later."

"Then we'll throw the coats on the floor," he said.

"Slob."

Two cans of beer in the kitchen. They stood in front of the gas stove. Terry Flynn turned the oven on and the heat warmed their legs. He turned on the gas burners and they alternately drank beer and held their hands over the blue flames. "See. A romantic fire, two cans of nectar of the gods. I'll be in your pants by morning."

"And all for little me," she said.

255

He grinned at her. If he did not love her, he thought, he would have asked her to marry him. But since he had been married once, he thought—objectively—that he was not very good at it. Besides, he told her once, they'd probably see less of each other if they were living in the same place.

"Remember Desmond Clayton? He dropped me a note. He's going to take a job with the *Washington Post*. Funny he'd drop me a note."

"You understood him."

"Some things. The day he saw that jiveass black messiah standing outside his apartment, he knew something. He knew he went to Harvard and his old man was in the UN but what it came down to was a jiveass piece of living scum like that black messiah telling him, 'Asshole, it don't matter, you still a nigger.' It scared the shit out of him because he was afraid that the messiah was right. I knew that. I knew where Desmond was coming from."

"Why? Who stands out there for you?" she said.

He was surprised and glanced quickly at her. "I don't know." He thought it over. "I thought it was Queeney. In a way. But now

that you ask, I guess it was Sid. Is Sid, since the son of a bitch is back."

"I don't understand."

"He blew it in California. He had a chance to get away. Pathetic. He comes back in three weeks. He's a fucking addict, he can't shake the habit. Cops. He wants to be back home with the cops. What the fuck is so great about being in this fucking city in the middle of winter in the middle of your life, being a cop? What is so fucking great about it? Why the fuck didn't Sid give it a chance?"

And he was not shouting when he said these things. He spoke softly.

Poor Terry Flynn, thought Karen Kovac, and she touched his large hand.

He grinned, the schoolboy ready for a new joke. "Wanna fuck?"

And she went to him.

And kissed him.

And held him.

A note on the text
Large print edition designed by
Bernadette Montalvo.
Composed in 16 pt Plantin
on a Xyvision 300/Linotron 202N
by Henry Elliott
of G.K. Hall & Co.

P9-BZS-309